TM

SUPERMAN
R E T U R N S™

THE JUNIOR NOVEL

Adapted by Louise Simonson

Screenplay by Michael Dougherty & Dan Harris

Story by Bryan Singer & Michael Dougherty
& Dan Harris

Superman created by Jerry Siegel and Joe Shuster

LITTLE, BROWN AND COMPANY
New York · Boston · London

Little, Brown and Company
1271 Avenue of the Americas, New York, NY 10020
Visit our Web site at www.lb-kids.com

First Edition: June 2006

LCCN: 2005937696
ISBN: 0-316-17805-5

10 9 8 7 6 5 4 3 2 1

COM-MO

Printed in the U.S.A.

Book design by Maria Mercado
The text was set in Bembo and the display type is Serpentine.

One

The ship was a shimmering crystal whirling through space. And in its sparkling center, Superman slept.

He was dressed in dark gray, so he would have been easy to spot, lying in suspended animation within his crystalline cold-sleep cocoon. But no one was there to look for him. Superman was alone. In some ways, he had been alone for almost all of his life.

As he slept, he dreamed . . .

&oo;   &oo;   &oo;

He was a baby, cradled in his father's arms.

Then an earthquake sent a shockwave through his world. The red sun flared — larger, brighter. But he wasn't afraid.

"Soon Krypton will be destroyed," his father said. "Despite

overwhelming evidence, my plea to evacuate this planet has been ignored. It leaves me no choice, Lara."

"But Jor-El, surely —" his mother pleaded.

Jor-El continued, "We must send our son, in this spaceship, to a far galaxy, to the planet Earth, in the hope that he will find a new home there."

"But why Earth, Jor-El? Its natives are primitives. Their science and culture are thousands of years behind ours."

Jor-El nodded. "That is true. The advantage will help him survive."

"He will be odd. Different," Lara argued.

"Earth's yellow sun will heighten his abilities," Jor-El countered. "He will be able to fly. He will be fast. And virtually invulnerable."

"Isolated, alone!" Lara said, reaching out for her infant son.

Another tremor struck, sending shards of crystal raining down on them. The ground shook convulsively.

Lara withdrew her arms and looked desperately at her husband's face.

Jor-El placed his son in an egg-shaped cradle, nestled in a ship of crystal.

"He will not be alone. He will never be alone." He held out

2

a crystal for Lara to see, then placed it in the cradle beside the infant.

He closed the hatch. "Sleep, my little Kal-El. You will travel far, but we will never leave you. Even in the face of our deaths, the richness of our lives will be yours."

The infant Kal-El felt the cold-sleep cradle rock as the ship carried him into space.

"All that I have learned, everything I feel, all of this and more I bequeath you, my son," his father's soothing voice came from the crystal. "Now close your eyes . . . and sleep."

And while the infant Kal-El slept, the red sun of Krypton exploded behind him.

⊷ ⊷ ⊷

Superman awoke to a jolting alarm and flashing lights. He had been dreaming . . . of Krypton.

The rounded top of his cold-sleep cocoon sprang open.

He sat up, feeling dizzy. He looked around the faceted interior of the crystal ship.

And he remembered.

⊷ ⊷ ⊷

He had been born on the planet Krypton weeks before that world was destroyed. But he had been raised on Earth.

He had tried to lead a normal life as reporter Clark Kent, while also acting as Superman, protector of his adopted world.

But he felt caught between his human surroundings and his Kryptonian heritage — different from everyone else in the universe and alone. Above all, he valued truth, and the fact that he was forced to live a double life — secret even from Lois Lane, the woman he had come to love — was tearing him apart.

Then an unmanned exploration satellite had picked up a steady signal coming from space. Earth's astronomers speculated that it was a distress call from a remnant of the destroyed planet, Krypton.

In the end, he realized that he needed to return to the planet of his birth, in order to understand who and what he truly was.

He told only his human mother he was leaving. After all, he didn't expect to be gone more than a few months.

He had flown into the stratosphere and absorbed the unimpeded rays from Earth's yellow sun that gave him superhuman *powers, to keep him strong for the long journey ahead. Then he had climbed into his crystal ship and left the Earth.*

He had traveled in suspended animation to avoid draining his energy. He would need to be at maximum ability to explore the remnants of his home world . . .

∞   ∞   ∞

Now, a surge of excitement filled him.

He staggered to the controls. At his command the ship's front wall became transparent.

Below him, a dark shape blotted out the stars. "Krypton," he breathed. "At last."

"Light!" he commanded, and a spotlight shone from the ship.

It refracted off cities made of crystal. But those crystals were dead, not glowing with energy like his spaceship.

He flew closer — listening for the reported signal with superhearing, using X-ray vision to scan the buildings for survivors.

He heard nothing. And saw, instead of survivors, an

eerie greenish glow. Radiation from the exploded red sun had transformed the crystals of his home world. They had become kryptonite — a deadly poison to Superman.

His stomach swirled. But he forced his ship down further, through a broken dome. Its spotlight lit a hieroglyph. Similar hieroglyphs were on the monuments nearby. Among them, he spotted his S-shield crest, the symbol of his Kryptonian heritage.

The nausea became crippling pain.

"Out!" he said. "Away!"

The ship obeyed. And, looking down, he realized he had been in the Kryptonian Valley of the Elders.

Then suddenly, the land ended — and beyond it were the stars. Was this shard of his home world all that was left?

As his ship pulled away, he saw giant slabs of kryptonite bursting through the planet's mantle.

"No wonder I'm feeling weak," he muttered. But he had been dizzy — muddleheaded — when he awoke. How long had his ship been circling, searching for signs of life? How long had he been away from Earth and its life-giving yellow sun?

"Charts," he said. A holographic array of stars and Kryptonian symbols flashed before him.

"No!" he muttered. "That's impossible." But he knew it wasn't. He had been away from Earth not for months, but for years. It had taken his ship that long to locate a piece of Krypton large enough to possibly sustain life.

Something large slammed into the crystal ship, nearly shaking Superman from his feet. Another jolt followed.

He looked out the transparent window and saw that he had sent the ship into an asteroid field of kryptonite.

Superman fell to his knees, clutching his abdomen.

A barrage of asteroids slammed into his ship. Giant chunks of his ship's crystals shattered and fell away. He knew the ship would grow replacement crystals. But that wouldn't . . . couldn't happen indefinitely.

Weakly, Superman croaked, "Earth! Return to Earth!"

He staggered toward his cold-sleep cocoon. As he collapsed into it, he looked not at the remnants of the destroyed planet of his birth, but at the holographic image of the world that had adopted him as its own son.

As the hatch closed over his cold-sleep cocoon, and the ship moved from the asteroid field and into open space, he had only one thought.

"Earth," he whispered. "Home."

TWO

"Alienation!" Martha Kent said, looking up from the Scrabble board. She tucked a strand of white-blonde hair behind her ear and grinned. "That's . . . seventy-four points. Which gives me 409 points to your 280. Want to concede now?"

As Ben Hubbard gave her a mock scowl, the lenses of his glasses caught the kitchen light. "You're not doing a very good job of letting me win."

"Humor me, Ben," she said. "I'll let you win when we're playing for a new —"

She stopped, head tilted, listening. *That sound,* she thought. *It's the same. I'll never forget —*

The Scrabble pieces on the board began to shake.

The ancient orange-and-tan dog lying on the floor lifted his head with a questioning whine.

"Martha —?" Ben began.

WHAM! A crash shook the house, rattling the windowpanes.

"Holy crow!" Ben grabbed for the phone. "Whatever that was, we need to call the sheriff!"

"It's all right, Ben." Gently Martha pried the phone from his fingers. "It's just a meteorite. Sometimes they burn up in the atmosphere and sometimes they make it all the way down. No need to trouble the sheriff about it."

Ben didn't look convinced.

"Listen, it's late," she said. "Thanks for dinner . . ."

Ben raised an eyebrow. "But —?"

"I'll see you tomorrow evening."

She waved from the kitchen porch until Ben's old truck turned onto the main road and rumbled out of sight.

Then she grabbed her jacket.

She climbed into her pickup truck, gunned the engine, and turned onto a dirt track that separated the fields.

Martha stopped the truck when she spotted a deep ditch across the road. She climbed down, shining a flashlight on the trench, and the light refracted from tiny shards of broken crystal.

Her heart beat faster.

She jogged beside the trench, through the corn stubble, until she reached a smoking crater. And there, half embedded in the dirt, was Clark's crystalline ship, still glowing with otherworldly energy.

"Clark!" she called frantically. "Son!"

She had begun to climb into the pit when he grabbed her shoulder.

"Mom," he whispered. And collapsed into her arms.

❧ ❧ ❧

In a luxurious mansion, in an exclusive suburb of Metropolis, a lonely and bitter old woman lay dying.

"Mom!" a man's voice called from beyond her locked bedroom door.

"Grandma!" a child wailed.

"Open this door!" a woman's voice ordered.

The old woman's little Yorkshire terrier whined and scratched at the door.

The man sitting beside her velvet-draped four-poster bed ignored her family's cries and angry hammering, as he ignored the beeps from the machine that was counting out her final heartbeats.

Old Gertrude Vanderworth smiled at the blond man fondly. "In spite of your past, I know you're a good man," she mumbled. "And you deserve a second chance. From the moment I received your first letter, I knew you weren't like the rest of those vultures.

"You promised if I helped you get out of prison, that you'd take care of me. And you have. Beautifully," she croaked.

The blond man smiled modestly and pushed the last will and testament across the satin sheets toward her. He placed a pen in her hand.

"And that's why you deserve what Stephen left me," she mumbled. "That's why you deserve everything."

She started to write her name on the will: *Gertrude Vander*

Her eyes closed. Her breathing stopped. The machine emitted a final wailing *beeeeep!*

No, the man thought. *Not now! Not when I'm so close!*

Before her hand could drop, he grabbed it roughly and scrawled the remainder of her signature.

He snatched up the will and opened the door with a flourish.

He swept the curly wig from his bald head and tossed it to the woman's son. "You can keep that," Lex Luthor sneered as he strode toward the front door. "Everything else is mine."

Three

The old hound whined. Then he barked, impatiently.

Clark opened his eyes. His bedroom curtains were fluttering in a light breeze, filtering early morning sunlight onto the braided rug beside his bed and the scarred dresser beyond.

He was home.

"Hey, boy," he said. "Need to go outside?"

The dog wagged his tail and paced stiffly to the bedroom door.

⁖ ⁖ ⁖

Dressed in jeans and a worn flannel shirt, Clark bounded downstairs with the dog at his heels. He stopped at a table, briefly studying the family photos arranged there. Clark was at the center of all of them —

a baby splashing in his bath, blowing out candles on his seventh birthday, driving the tractor for the first time, graduating from high school.

The dog whined again and Clark headed for the kitchen door.

"Five years," he thought. "I've been gone . . . asleep . . . for five whole years!"

He looked at the rusted machinery, the neglected fields. During the time he was gone, the farm had fallen into disrepair.

The old hound nudged Clark's hand and Clark stroked his head, struck suddenly by the gray in the dog's muzzle.

He remembered the day he'd gotten the dog. His twelfth birthday. The day . . .

⊷   ⊷   ⊷

Clark was running through the cornfield, the puppy at his heels, so fast it felt like he was flying.

Then, incredibly, he was flying. He looked down at the ground in alarm. Then up again. The barn roof was coming up fast. He covered his face, bracing for the impact. For jarring pain.

He crashed through the roof. And felt nothing. He was in-side the barn, hovering in midair, and everything around him was a blur.

My glasses, he thought, in confusion. *I must have dropped them when I . . . hit. He squinted at the barn floor, trying to spot them.*

To his surprise, the floor came into focus.

Then he was looking through it, at what lay beyond. A cellar, holding an egg-shaped object the size of a cradle.

Clark landed on the barn floor with a thump. He wrenched open the cellar door and leaped inside. He touched the egg and a panel in its oval surface slid open. In it was a large crystal, maybe a foot long, resting on a blanket.

Clark picked it up. At his touch, the crystal glowed with light.

⸎   ⸎   ⸎

That day was like a dream, Clark thought as he wandered toward the barn. The beginning of his knowledge about who he was . . . and what he was. Different. And alone.

In a corner of the barn, Martha had stacked five years' worth of *Daily Planet* newspapers.

Clark smiled.

At superspeed, he scanned the headlines: ASTRON-OMERS RECEIVE SIGNAL FROM DESTROYED PLANET: IS THERE LIFE ON KRYPTON? Then, SUPERMAN DISAPPEARS.

Headlines followed, detailing disasters made by man and by nature. At first, they spoke wistfully of Super-man, asking: WHERE HAS HE GONE? And WILL HE EVER RETURN?

Then other news pushed Superman's disappearance from the front page.

And then, not even a year ago, an editorial ap-peared.

WHY THE WORLD DOESN'T NEED SUPERMAN

By Lois Lane

For five long years, humanity has stared into the sky, wait-ing, hoping and praying for Superman's return. We have spent

our days asking where he went, debated why he left, and wondered if he's even alive . . .

Clark scanned the rest until he reached the final paragraphs . . .

People have always longed for gods, messiahs, and saviors to swoop down from the sky and deliver them from their troubles. But in the end, these saviors always leave and we are faced with the same troubles that were there from the beginning.

So instead of facing them ourselves, we wait for the savior to return. But the savior never does. And we realize it was better had he never come at all.

∞   ∞   ∞

That night, Clark sat at the kitchen table staring at the yellowed newspaper.

The evening news shows were on the TV.

"In yet another nighttime siege of a Chicago bank, armed robbers evaded capture by —"

Clark hit the remote — *Click!* "A tornado ripped through a town . . ."

Click!

"A family was held at gunpoint . . ."

Click!

"A highrise erupted in flames . . ."

Clark had always known he could never stop all the bad things from happening. He was just one man, even if he was Superman. But he had done some good. And, he had to admit, he'd taken solace in that feeling of being needed.

Now, Lois's article was telling him that, without hope of his intervention, people would solve their own problems. If that was true, the world probably *was* better off without him.

They'd certainly survived his five-year absence. Discouraged, Clark clicked off the TV.

"Clark, could you reheat my cup?" his mom called from the laundry room.

"Sure," Clark said. He stared at the cup and, for an instant, his eyes glowed red. The coffee began to steam. *That's me, the human microwave*, Clark thought. *Saving the world, one cup of coffee at a time.*

"Feeling better?" Martha plonked the laundry basket on a chair.

"Getting there," Clark said. "Don't worry about the ship — I buried it this morning." He looked up and saw that Martha's eyes were filled with tears.

"Mom?" he said, worried. "What is it?"

Martha swiped at her cheeks and smiled. "It's just . . . you were gone for so long, I was afraid that . . . Did you find what you were looking for?"

"No," Clark said. "I thought . . . hoped . . . it might still be —"

"Your home?" Martha asked.

"This is my home," Clark told her. "That place was a graveyard. I'm all that's left."

Martha sat at the table across from him and covered one of his large hands with her own. "The universe is a big place. You never know who's out there. And even if you are the last — it doesn't mean you're alone."

Clark sighed. "I know."

Martha sipped her coffee. She pulled an earring from her apron pocket and began to put it on. "When are you heading to Metropolis?"

Clark shrugged. "Actually, I was thinking of sticking around the farm. It wouldn't take much time for me to repaint the barn, replant the fields . . ."

Martha's purse was lying on the chair. She felt in it for her compact and pink lipstick, and then began to put lipstick on. "What about that girl you used to like — Lois Lane? The one you had me send all those postcards to?"

Clark glanced at the paper beside him on the table. "It's been five years . . ."

Martha followed his gaze. "Since you've been gone, the news hasn't been quite what it used to be. The world can always use . . . more good reporters."

Clark stood restlessly. "I'm not sure they'd *want* me back."

Martha said firmly, "Your father used to say that you were put here for a reason. And we both know it wasn't to work on a farm."

There was a knock at the kitchen door. Clark and Martha turned as Ben Hubbard stuck his head inside. "Martha?"

Martha smiled. "Ben. Come in."

Ben handed Martha a dozen red roses. He kissed her cheek.

Martha smiled. "Ben, you remember my son, Clark. He's here for a . . . short visit!"

Warily, Clark shook Ben's hand.

"Ben's taking me into town for dinner," Martha said, as she filled a vase with water.

"To celebrate," Ben continued. "We've been engaged a month now."

Clark blinked. "You two . . . you're —?"

Martha glanced at Ben.

"I'll . . . uh . . . just wait . . . in the truck," Ben said. He backed out through the kitchen door and closed it softly behind him.

Martha cupped Clark's cheek in her callused palm. "Clark, dear, no one will ever replace your father. But Ben and I have found something special. Together. And, well, this might come as a shock, but I . . . I'm selling the farm. Ben and I are getting married . . . and moving to Montana."

"Montana?!?" Clark sat down heavily.

"We . . . love the fishing there. It's been a long time

since your father died. Things change. People need to move on. Not even you can stop the world from spinning. We'll talk more tomorrow." She kissed his forehead. "Don't wait up."

⊶   ⊶   ⊶

Clark watched his mother climb into the cab of Ben's freshly polished truck.

"Five years." Clark sighed. "I've been away five years."

Four

The sharp bow of the *Gertrude* broke through thin sheets of ice as it sliced through Arctic waves.

Everything about the yacht was luxurious. Its lower deck had a swimming pool. The mid-deck held the private master's quarters and the main gallery with high ceilings, huge windows, office equipment, a pool table, and a grand piano. It even had a kitchen and pantry worthy of a five-star restaurant. The topmost deck featured a helipad with a private helicopter.

Yes, the Gertrude *is extraordinary,* Lex Luthor thought, as he settled more comfortably on the Italian leather couch in the main gallery. But that was as it should be. The yacht belonged to him, now. And Lex Luthor was no ordinary man.

He straightened his sober black toupee, then scanned another glossy page of *Crystals: The Definitive Guide*.

Das Rheingold, by Wagner, thundered from the sound system, obscuring the knock on the gallery door and muffling the hesitant "Mr. Luthor? Sir?"

The door opened a crack. Grant entered, high-tech binoculars hanging from a strap around his pudgy neck. Behind him came Riley, a thin weasel-like man wielding a video camera.

"Mr. Luthor? Sir?" Grant said again.

The striking dark-haired woman at the bar looked up from mixing drinks. Riley pointed the camera in her direction. "Your *friends* give me the creeps, Lex," she said.

Luthor shrugged. "Prison is a creepy place, Kitty. One needs creepy friends, in order to survive."

He turned to the pudgy little man. "What is it, Grant?"

Grant's eyes were shining with excitement. "We found it!"

Luthor smiled. "Drop anchor."

Bundled in Arctic-weather gear, Lex Luthor led his crew away from the helicopter resting on the ice shelf and into a swirl of snow. Kitty Kowalski, swaddled in furs, walked beside him. Grant, Riley (with his camcorder), brainy Stanford, and hulking Brutus trudged after them, squinting through their snow goggles, looking cold and miserable.

Stanford stopped and raised his high-tech binoculars. "You were right," he shouted over the roar of the wind. "There's an unnatural weather pattern keeping it hidden."

Luthor smiled coldly. "I'm always right."

"So now that we're out in the middle of nowhere, away from prying ears, does the finest criminal mind of our time think I'm worthy of hearing his plan?" Kitty said.

"Do you know the story of Prometheus?" Luthor asked. He glanced at her blank expression and shrugged. "Of course you don't. Prometheus was a god who stole the power of fire from the other gods and gave control of it to mortals. In essence, he gave us technology. He gave us power."

Kitty looked at Luthor as if he had lost his mind. "So we're stealing fire. In the Arctic?" she said.

"In a way."

They climbed a slope and a cathedral-like structure loomed before them, made of massive crystals soaring out of the ice.

"Ah!" Luthor's voice was laced with satisfaction. "*This* is the alien technology that created the constantly swirling storm that led me here."

⊷　⊷　⊷

Looking up, not watching his step, Grant tripped and slammed into a column. "This ice . . . it's warm," Grant said.

"It isn't ice," Luthor told him absently.

Walking between towering crystal columns, they entered the structure. Its central chamber was a breathtaking combination of walls, consoles, and strange equipment, all made of crystals that caught and refracted the light.

Luthor removed his goggles and pulled off his gloves.

Riley gazed around in wonder. "Was this . . . Superman's house?" he whispered hoarsely.

"You might think that," Luthor said. "But, no, he lived among us. This is more a monument to a long-dead and extremely powerful civilization."

Luthor snapped his fingers and Riley resumed filming.

Luthor studied the central hall, then sauntered toward an adjoining chamber. Pulling off her own goggles, Kitty trailed after him.

A large section of the wall was missing, as if a crystal that had grown there had broken off.

"What's this, his garage?" Kitty asked.

"In a way," Luthor murmured. "The leading theory is that Superman left Earth in a futile attempt to find his home world. If so, even Superman would have to rely on a craft of some kind. I'll bet Gertrude's last dollar that's exactly what used to be here."

Behind him, Stanford stifled a laugh.

Kitty looked at Luthor suspiciously. "And he decided to leave, all on his own?"

Luthor glanced at Stanford. "Well . . . we gave him a little push."

Luthor returned to the main chamber. He ran his hand over the rows of crystals on top of the central console. "Let's see how it reacts to heat."

As if Luthor's touch had thrown a switch, the entire console began to glow. Some of the crystals rose. Others fell. And in the center of the console, the foot-long Master Crystal glowed brighter than the rest.

Experimentally, Luthor removed the Master Crystal and placed it in the largest slot in the console.

Suddenly, shafts of light lit the fortress and whispers echoed all around them. Then, within the crystal walls, the light became multiple images of a white-haired man in a long tunic. A voice said, "My son!"

"That's Superman's father?" Kitty took a step backward. Luthor's henchmen edged nervously toward the center of the chamber.

"Over the years I have instructed you in all the languages, arts, and sciences of Earth, as well as of your home world, Krypton. There are, no doubt, more questions to be asked," the shining figure continued.

"Can he see us?" Kitty whispered.

"No, it's just a recording." Luthor waved his hand through one of the images, distorting the light. "It thinks I'm him."

Kitty shivered. "Lex, I'm cold."

"Shut up and get comfortable," Luthor snapped. "We're going to be here for a while."

"So, my son. Speak," the Kryptonian figure continued.

Luthor looked around at the gleaming, multifaceted chamber and smiled in triumph. "Tell me everything," he commanded. "But first, tell me about crystals."

Five

The yellow cab stopped in front of the entrance to the Daily Planet building.

As Clark Kent climbed from the backseat, reaching for his wallet, the cab driver popped the trunk and walked around to the back. He tried to remove the suitcases but they wouldn't budge. "Whaddya got in these things, bricks?"

Clark paid him, then picked up the suitcases easily. The cab driver gaped. Clark shrugged. "I've been working out."

Clark stared up at the metal globe, the symbol of the newspaper, spinning atop the building. Then he carried his suitcases through the brass-edged doors and into the marble lobby.

He hadn't told anyone but Editor in Chief Perry

White that he was returning to Metropolis. After he had left the paper so abruptly, he felt lucky Perry had given him another job.

Home, Clark thought, as he rode up to the paper's bullpen. *Metropolis and the* Daily Planet *are as much my home as Smallville.* More, he realized with a slightly sick feeling, now that his mother was selling the farm.

The bullpen looked much as it had looked when he left — a long, narrow room, lined with old-fashioned windows that actually opened. Perry White's office was still at the end.

Circular pillars reached from floor to ceiling. The space was crowded with desks and chairs. Stacks of papers littered most desktops. Some reporters typed at their computers. Others were bustling in or out on assignment.

But there were differences. In the past five years, the Planet had switched from desktop computers to sleek laptop models. Large flat-screen monitors were mounted on the pillars, showing breaking news from stations around the world. While Superman slept in space, technology on Earth had advanced.

As Clark carried his suitcases down the central aisle, he swiveled his head, searching for familiar faces. For Lois.

She wasn't at her desk. He stifled his disappointment.

His heavy suitcase slammed into a desk, bumping a camera hanging off the edge. Dropping a suitcase, Clark grabbed the camera at superspeed before it could smash onto the floor.

"Hey! Careful!" said a voice behind him.

Clark turned. A huge grin split his face. "Sorry, Jimmy," he said. He placed the camera safely in the center of the desk.

"Mr. Clark! I mean, Kent. Mr. Kent," Jimmy Olsen stammered excitedly. "Oh, wow! Welcome back! Hey, come with me. No, wait. Don't move! Stay here!"

Before Clark could say, "Just call me Clark," Jimmy had bolted off toward the tiny snack room.

Clark stood as directed, staring after him. Since Clark had left, the young photographer had become a man, but he hadn't lost his enthusiasm. Clark grinned and lurched aside as two reporters nearly tripped over his suitcases.

"Sorry, guys," Clark said, shoving the suitcases closer

to Jimmy's desk. "Still looking for a place to live. If you know of anything reasonable . . ."

Without a word, the reporters, new guys Clark had never met, shoved past him and dashed for the bullpen's swinging doors.

"Here, Mr. Kent!" Jimmy handed Clark a foil-covered plate. "I made it myself."

Clark peeled back the aluminum. Beneath was an iced cake. Except slices had been dug out of it and its frosting had been smeared. Letters on top read:

WE COM ACK LARK

Jimmy sighed, disappointed. "I guess the guys got hungry."

"It'll still taste great! Thanks, Jimmy!" Clark said. And he thought, *At least someone's happy I'm back.*

⊶ ⊶ ⊶

"Olsen!" Perry White growled as he stalked up the aisle. "Where are those photos from the 66th Street birthday-clown massacre?"

Jimmy snapped to attention. "Being developed. Have 'em for you right away, Chief," he said. "Hey, look who's here!"

"Kent?" The gray-haired editor in chief turned to look Clark over. They shook hands.

"Hey Chief. Thanks for giving me my job back," Clark told him.

"Don't thank me," Perry muttered. "Thank Jack Green for dying!"

Clark smiled. "Well, I do appreciate it, Ch —"

"And don't call me Chief!" Perry growled and stalked back to his office.

Jimmy reached for Clark's suitcases. "Come on, let's get you set up —"

THUD! Jimmy was nearly floored by their weight. Using both arms, he began to drag one of them toward a far corner. Then he noticed that Clark was walking in the opposite direction, toward his old desk next to Lois's.

"Mr. Kent?" Jimmy shouted. Clark turned. Jimmy motioned toward the far corner of the room.

Confused, Clark turned and followed him, carrying a suitcase and the cake.

"So, wow, you sure are lucky. Hitting the open road and hitchhiking around the world. I can't wait to hear all about the Peruvian llama rodeo. I kept all the post-cards you sent."

Jimmy stopped before a small desk, in the farthest corner. "You've got Jack Green's old desk. Hey, gotta run. Those clown photos. I'll check on you in a bit, okay?"

"Say, do you know where I can find —" *Lois,* Clark thought. But Jimmy was already gone.

On the corner of Clark's new desk was a huge pile of papers. He leafed through them. They were obituaries — of people who hadn't died yet. The lowest assignment of the low. His new job.

Clark put down his half-eaten cake. *I guess Perry was a bit annoyed with how I left the paper after all,* he thought.

The good news was, the janitor's closet was right behind his new desk.

Making sure no one was watching, he snatched up his suitcases, carried them into the closet, and pulled the door shut behind him. He put one suitcase on a small table and opened it. Reaching beneath the pressed suits, shirts, and books, he pulled out a framed photo of his parents.

Beneath that was his blue Superman suit. He traced the S-shield with an index finger. He wasn't wearing it beneath his clothing. Lois had made it clear that Superman's help was no longer needed.

Resolutely, he shut the suitcase and stowed it behind a storage cabinet, out of sight.

From the bull pen, he heard Jimmy's voice call, "Mr. Kent! Where are you? Look — it's Lois!"

Lois!

Clark brushed back his hair, took a deep breath, and stepped into the bullpen.

Six

Jimmy and a balding reporter named Gil were staring up at one of the flat-screen monitors. "See? There she is!" Jimmy said, pointing. "In the second row, on the aisle. They just took off from Metropolis Bay Air Force Base."

Clark realized he was looking at a live feed of a press conference on board a specially outfitted Boeing 777. The reporters were there to cover the first launch of an orbital space shuttle using onboard solid rocket boosters instead of the usual external fuel tank. Adding to the drama, the shuttle would launch from the back of the same Boeing 777 in which the reporters were riding.

The monitor shifted focus to an attractive blonde at the front of the plane. She was standing before a screen showing the Boeing jet with the space shuttle, *Explorer,* piggybacked on top.

"The woman is Bobbie-Faye," Jimmy told Clark. "She's the NASA spokesperson."

"In the past, the space shuttle needed twelve million pounds of thrust just in its initial launch phase," Bobbie-Faye was saying. "By piggybacking the *Explorer* on this Boeing 777 —"

On the screen, Lois's hand shot up. Bobbie-Faye nodded.

"Lois Lane, *Daily Planet,*" Lois said. "You mentioned earlier that the *Explorer* will save taxpayers millions. But isn't it true that the cost of development was nine-hundred million dollars over budget and that the per-unit cost of each craft is almost double that of the original shuttle?"

Bobbie-Faye looked like she had bitten into something sour. "Why don't we save those questions for our post-launch briefing, Miss Lane?" she snapped.

"Go, Lois," Jimmy chortled.

"With all the noise you're making, I can't hear," Gil grumbled. "Turn it up, Olsen!"

Jimmy hit a button on the remote. The TV switched to a baseball game.

"Olsen, what're you doing?" Gil shrieked.

"Sorry. Sorry." As Jimmy frantically clicked buttons, trying to switch the channel back, Clark wandered over to Lois's desk. Its top was littered with files, papers, and old coffee cups. Clark smiled. He may have been gone five years, but that mess was eternal.

An open invitation to the Pulitzer Prize Awards ceremony had been tossed carelessly to one side. From his earlier scan of the *Daily Planet* newspapers, Clark knew Lois had won an award for her WHY THE WORLD DOESN'T NEED SUPERMAN editorial. Clark sighed. The fact that the Pulitzer committee backed her up had helped convince him that retiring Superman was the right thing to do.

Then, amid the clutter, Clark noticed a framed photo of Lois standing beside a handsome dark-haired man. They were holding the hands of a small dark-haired boy. Who was the dark-haired man? Who was the boy?

Searching for answers, Clark spotted another picture, half buried in the debris on Lois's desk. It was a crayon drawing of a house with smoke coming from the chimney. Along the top, in a young child's careful scrawl, were the words TO MOM. At the bottom of the picture was the name Jason.

Clark snatched up the photo and studied it anxiously.

"He looks older now," Jimmy said, peering over Clark's shoulder. "Kids grow up so fast. He's starting to look like his mother. Already takes after her, too, especially when it comes to getting into trouble."

"His . . . mother?" Clark asked.

"Oh, gee. Oh no. You've been gone," Jimmy sputtered. "Fearless reporter Lois Lane is a mommy. But I'm surprised she never told you."

"I haven't really been reachable," Clark said in a strangled voice. "Wait. She's married?"

"Yup. Well, not exactly," Jimmy said, confused about how to explain. "More like a prolonged engagement. But don't ask Miss Lane when they're tying the knot. She hates that question."

Carefully, Clark set the photograph back on Lois's desk.

"Clark, are you all right?" Jimmy asked. "Listen, why don't we grab some lunch?"

Jimmy tried hard to distract Clark, but there was no escaping Lois.

The TV at the restaurant, tuned to the shuttle launch, was showing an animated demonstration of the upcoming separation of the Boeing 777 and the piggybacked shuttle.

Bobbie-Faye's chirpy voice was saying ". . . Now, when we hit forty-thousand feet, the shuttle will detach, ascend, and then fire the first of two propellant systems, the liquid fuel boosters. Then, when the shuttle reaches the stratosphere, the orbital insertion boosters will fire, rocketing the craft into orbit and leaving behind a sort of 'magical rainbow' trail."

The TV cut back to Bobbie-Faye and the press corp. Lois had raised her hand. "Magical rainbow . . . ?" Lois asked. "That's a . . . *technical* term?"

Bobbie-Faye frowned. "It's an analogy, Miss Lane."

"Right," Lois snorted. "Of course."

The screen cut to a picture of the jet with its attached shuttle and two F-35 fighter jets flying escort.

Clark sighed. "Things change. I know they do. But . . . Lois. A woman like her . . . I thought she'd never settle down."

Jimmy shrugged. "If you ask me, I think she's still in love with you-know-who . . ."

Clark *knew* who — *Superman*. But Superman wasn't coming back.

Clark put his chin on his hand and sighed.

Seven

The burglar alarm beeped and Gertrude's small terrier barked as Lex Luthor stepped through the front door of the sprawling Vanderworth mansion. Kitty Kowalski, draped in jewelry, followed. Stanford, Grant, Brutus, and Riley, with his camcorder, trooped after her.

"Where is everyone?" Kitty asked.

"I've given the servants the day off," Luthor said.

Kitty wrinkled her nose. "This place is so tacky. Lex, why are we back here?"

Lex punched in the code that deactivated the alarm. "Because, while you were having your nails done, I was unlocking the secrets of one of the most advanced civilizations in the universe. You see, unlike our clunky Earth-bound methods of construction, the technology of Krypton — Superman's home world — was based on manipulating crystals."

Kitty shrugged. "Sounds like hocus-pocus to me."

Luthor smiled as he led the others down a hall, through a door, and into the basement. "Cities. Vehicles. Weapons. Entire continents. All can be grown! To think, one could create a new world with such a simple little object."

With a flourish, Luthor pulled the Kryptonian Master Crystal from his jacket pocket. "It's like a seed," he said. "All it needs is water."

Luthor flipped a switch on the basement wall. Spotlights illuminated a massive model train display, arranged on specially built tables around the basement.

"Wow!" Grant said. "Some setup! Hey, it's Metropolis! The city and the outer boroughs. Roads. Bridges. Train tracks. Look, the trains are moving."

Kitty stepped closer, interested in spite of herself. "The rivers even have little boats! They're moving, too."

"That's because there's real water," Grant enthused.

"And look — there's the Vanderworth mansion, right on the bay!"

While Kitty and Grant admired the miniature Metropolis, Stanford sat hunched over a workbench, studying the Kryptonian Master Crystal through a microscope. Luthor hovered beside him.

Finally, Stanford picked up a scalpel.

"Careful . . . careful," Luthor muttered.

Stanford began to scrape the edge of the Master Crystal. An inch–long sliver peeled off.

Gingerly, Stanford took calipers and lifted the tiny splinter.

Kitty peered over Lex's shoulder. "It's so small," she said.

"It's not the size that matters," Lex said. "Riley, are you getting this?"

Riley aimed the camcorder at the tiny shard.

"Do it," Lex told Stanford.

Stanford carried the sliver of crystal toward the model of Metropolis. He plunged it into the water of the miniature bay.

Nothing happened.

"Wow. That's really something, Lex," Kitty said sarcastically.

Luthor held up a finger. "Wait for it," he said.

Suddenly, the model trains began to slow.

Then the lights in the Vanderworth mansion went out, plunging the basement into darkness.

⚭   ⚭   ⚭

In a spreading wave across the city, electricity shut off. Traffic signals flickered out. Subway trains rolled to a standstill. The globe atop the Daily Planet building stopped midspin.

In the restaurant where Jimmy and Clark were eating, the lights and television blinked off.

Jimmy frowned. "Must be a blackout."

"Maybe." Clark pulled down his glasses and peered through the wall with X-ray vision. Outside on the street, the traffic had slowed to a stop. A normal blackout didn't affect car engines. Something else was going on.

⚭   ⚭   ⚭

High above the Atlantic, on board the Boeing 777, the screen beside Bobbie-Faye was showing the jet with its piggybacked shuttle in mid-flight. The shuttle commander's voice was saying, "Mission Control, booster ignition is at T-minus one minute and we are prepping to disengage couplings —"

Then the display screen in the cabin went blank and all the lights — in the jet and in the shuttle — cut off.

The jet engine slowed . . . and died.

The jet lurched downward.

We're losing altitude, Lois thought. *We're going to crash.*

Then, as suddenly as they had stopped, the jet's engines started again. And the Boeing 777 leveled off.

The interior lights in the press cabin came on, and the screen behind Bobbie-Faye flashed the image of the jet and shuttle.

This was more than a glitch, Lois realized. It was a system failure.

She sat back and waited for the news that the launch would be aborted.

In the restaurant where Clark and Jimmy were eating, the lights blinked on and the TV continued its coverage of the shuttle launch. The reporter's voice was rapid and concerned.

Across Metropolis, buses and cars began to move. Traffic signals blinked red and green and yellow. Trains rolled. The Daily Planet globe began to spin.

Once again, Metropolis had full power.

∞　　∞　　∞

The Vanderworth Mansion basement went from totally dark to glaringly bright, as floodlights once again lit the model city.

"Camera's working again, too," Riley muttered.

"Lucky us," Kitty muttered. "That's it?"

"Nope," Luthor said. "Riley, keep the camcorder focused on the bay!"

As Riley aimed his camera, the huge table beneath the miniature Metropolis began to shake. Cracks formed in the landscape as the model city began to break apart. Tiny bridges collapsed. Tracks split. Trains crashed. Buildings toppled.

Then the basement surrounding them began to shake. Pipes burst, spraying water everywhere. Cracks traveled up the walls and through the ceiling.

BOOM! Something crashed overhead.

The floodlights exploded, raining down glass.

Kitty and Luthor's henchmen braced themselves for utter blackness. But an eerie glow from the miniature bay lit the ruined basement.

And the sliver of submerged crystal began to grow.

"Amazing," Luthor murmured into the shuddering gloom. "Simply . . . amazing!"

As Lois had expected, the voice of the Mission Control flight director came over the speakers in the press cabin: "Shuttle commander, not sure what just happened. But we're going to have to scrub the launch."

Lois nodded. She watched the simulcast video footage, shot from one of the escort planes, as the Boeing 777 banked westward, returning the piggybacked shuttle to the Metropolis Bay Air Force Base.

"Copy that," the shuttle commander said. "Aborting

booster ignition." A second later, his voice said, "Mission Control, boosters are not responding. We are still counting down for ignition."

"Can you release the couplings?" Mission Control asked.

Lois heard a series of loud pops overhead.

"That is a negative, sir," the shuttle commander said. "Couplings have fired but have not disengaged. We have a malfunction. Automatic countdown to launch continuing. Can you do a remote override?"

"Negative, *Explorer*," the flight director said, an edge of panic in his voice. "Override not responding."

Overhead, the shuttle booster rumbled and shook.

BOOM! The press cabin lurched forward as a deafening roar drowned out the Shuttle commander's voice coming over the speakers, announcing, "Primary boosters have fired."

Bobbie-Faye, at the front of the cabin, was thrown to the floor.

Lois was pinned to her seat by the g-force. *The shuttle is still attached*, she thought. *The blast will melt the tail section. And with our added weight, the shuttle can carry us up only so far . . . then gravity will pull the jet and shuttle back toward the ground.*

"Aviation disaster of the century," she muttered. "And I won't be alive to write the story."

She thought about her son at preschool. She hoped his class wasn't watching the launch. Jason was bright. He would understand what was happening. She didn't want her son to see her die.

Eight

The news flashed around the world — the first flight of the shuttle *Explorer* was experiencing serious technical difficulties. The shuttle's boosters had fired before detaching from the jet. Both craft had veered dramatically off course and out of control.

❦   ❦   ❦

Seated in the booth at the diner, Jimmy stared up at the TV screen in horror.

"Clark!" Jimmy said. "Lois is on that plane." He looked across the table.

There was a wad of money next to Clark's half-eaten sandwich. But Clark was gone.

❦   ❦   ❦

In the cabin of the Boeing 777, oxygen masks dropped from the ceiling. That meant the cabin was losing pressure, Lois knew. The oxygen supply had been compromised.

As she reached for her oxygen mask, she glanced around.

The only person not buckled into a seat was Bobbie-Faye, who was trying to crawl toward the empty seat in front of Lois.

Leaving her oxygen mask dangling, Lois unsnapped her seat belt. Holding tightly to the armrest of her seat with one hand, she fought the crushing g-force to reach forward as far as she could.

Over the still–operational intercom, the shuttle pilot's voice said, "Entering stratosphere in sixteen seconds."

Lois grabbed Bobbie-Faye's wrist. With all her might, Lois hauled the woman forward, until Bobbie-Faye was able to grab the arm of her own seat and collapse into it.

Still straining forward, Lois pulled Bobbie-Faye's oxygen mask down, clamped it over her nose, and tightened the elastic back behind her head.

Somewhat revived, Bobbie-Faye fumbled for her seat belt.

Only then did Lois collapse back into her own seat, put on her own oxygen mask, and rebuckle her belt. She tried to breathe deeply and stay calm, as she faced the certainty of her own death.

Clark dashed down the sidewalk, past people gathered in front of electronics stores, watching the disaster unfold on TV.

He slipped into an alley, ripped open his shirt — and remembered that he had decided that he would no longer be Superman. His suit was in his suitcase at the Daily Planet building.

He glanced skyward. High above Metropolis, a jet filled with reporters was in desperate trouble. And unless he did something, all of them — including Lois — would die.

His father — his human father — had told him he was put on Earth for a reason. And, suddenly, he knew that his father had been right.

He was going to save them, despite Lois's article, and despite the fact that the Pulitzer committee had agreed with her.

∞   ∞   ∞

Moving at superspeed — too fast for the naked eye to see — Clark raced around the corner and into the Daily Planet Building. He dove into a miraculously empty elevator, shoved aside the ceiling panels, and flew up the elevator shaft.

Hovering on the eighteenth floor, he swept the hall and bullpen beyond with X-ray vision. The few reporters who hadn't gone out to lunch were clustered around the TV monitors.

Clark forced the elevator doors open using superstrength. Before the elevator doors had shut behind him, Clark was down the hall, in the bullpen, then inside the supply closet.

Still moving at superspeed, he pulled out his suitcase, yanked it open, and pulled on his blue and red Superman suit. He tossed his glasses aside.

He glanced through the door with X-ray vision. The reporters were still staring at the monitors. On the screen, an anchorman was saying that the attached ships had just entered the stratosphere.

Superman stepped out of the supply closet. Two steps at superspeed carried him to an open window.

Then *VOOSH!* Superman was in the air. Metropolis stretched below him. He scanned the sky, then soared upward.

Superman had returned.

Above, he spotted the escort jets. They had fallen behind the shuttle, which was swiftly approaching the mesosphere.

Superman flew past them.

Up ahead was the Boeing 777, with the shuttle still attached.

With superhearing, Superman heard the shuttle commander say, "Booster is counting. 5 . . . 4 . . . 3 . . . 2 . . ."

Superman had almost reached the jet when the secondary booster fired. The blast knocked Superman backward, even as it blew the tail section off the jet.

The shuttle rocketed toward space, dragging the Boeing 777 with it.

Superman raced after them.

⟡ ⟡ ⟡

Lois felt the blast of heat, then the lurch forward. The cabin trembled. Frost began to form on exposed surfaces.

Lois understood all too well what was happening. A commercial jet wasn't built to take this kind of punishment. It was bound to shake apart.

Fighting the g-force, Lois forced her head around to look out the window. She saw the blue sky fading into black. And then she saw the stars. Bright. Beautiful. And, in that moment of weakness, her last thoughts turned to *him*.

Five years ago, Superman had disappeared from Earth. Despite the lack of any supporting evidence, speculation was that he had gone back where he came from — to live among the stars. Lois wished —

A blue and red blur zipped past the window. Lois

blinked and felt a surge of hope. It had looked like —
but no, that was impossible.

∞   ∞   ∞

Superman landed on the roof of the jet.

He squeezed his body between it and the shuttle and
pressed upward, forcing the attached craft apart. The
couplings snapped off, shuttle and jet separated, and
the jet fell away.

Swiftly calculating force and angle, Superman
grabbed the bottom of the shuttle with two hands.
Using superstrength, he shoved the shuttle, sending it
flying faster and higher. *Just like sailing a paper airplane,*
Superman thought.

Then he dove for the plummeting jet, though his
superhearing was still focused on the shuttle *Explorer.*
"Mission Control, do you read?" he heard the shuttle
commander say. "We're in orbit. Everything is . . . okay."

Moving at superspeed, Superman plunged past the
falling jet.

Below, he saw a stadium filled with people. A baseball

game had been in progress, but now the audience was screaming in panic, scrambling madly to escape.

Superman came up under the nose of the jet. He put his hands out and shoved.

The jet slowed. It slid past the scoreboard.

Superman gave one final push and the plane stopped — a few feet over home plate.

Superman lowered the jet, slowly and carefully, onto the field as the audience stared in awestruck silence. Superman could hear their whispers: "It's Superman! He's back! Superman has returned!"

Hovering beside the damaged fuselage, Superman ripped the passenger door off its hinges and tossed it near first base. He stepped into the cabin.

"Is everyone all right?" he asked.

The reporters all nodded numbly.

"I suggest you all stay in your seats until medical attention arrives," he said.

Lois leaned out from her seat in the second row to look at him. He started toward her eagerly, then stopped, concerned by the shock on her face.

And, once again, it struck him how long he'd been away.

"Are you okay?" he asked Lois.

Lois squeaked.

Superman smiled.

Then he remembered the other reporters and realized they were staring. He stepped away from Lois and faced the cabin.

"Well, I hope this little incident hasn't put any of you off flying," he said. "Statistically speaking, it's still the safest way to travel."

Superman turned and walked up the aisle. He looked back, a single glance at Lois. Then he gazed out over the baseball stadium.

The audience began to applaud . . . a few claps at first that became a clamor and then a roar.

Superman leaped into the air.

Lois staggered to the open door and leaned out. She watched Superman until he was out of sight.

Nine

The basement of the Vanderworth estate was a ruin of dripping pipes and cracked walls, all lit by an eerie, greenish glow.

Luthor glanced at Riley. "Did you get that?"

Riley still had his camera pointed at the remains of the model city. "Yeah," he said. "I got the whole scary thing."

Luthor gazed at the destroyed model city and the crystal edifice that had grown up through it and down beneath the table.

It's nearly identical to Superman's crystal fortress, Luthor thought with satisfaction.

⤜⧫⤛   ⤜⧫⤛   ⤜⧫⤛

"I want to know it all," Perry White growled. "I want to know everything."

The late afternoon sun, slanting through the windows of the Daily Planet conference room, cast long shadows as Perry paced before his staff. The men and women sitting at the long conference table practically quivered with the excitement of covering a major breaking story. Only Lois, jotting notes on a yellow pad, seemed indifferent to what Perry was saying.

Clark glanced at her. Except for a vague smile in his direction when she'd entered the room, Lois hadn't looked at him.

Perry glared at Jimmy. "Olsen, you haven't taken a decent shot in two months! I want photos of Superman — bathed in stadium lights, flying into the sunset, whatever!"

He turned to a dark-haired man. "Sports: How will this event change baseball? How will they get the plane out of there?"

He whirled on a plump woman. "Travel: Where did he go? Was he on vacation? If so, where?"

He leaned on the table. "Get me answers, people. In time for the morning edition!"

The staff rushed from the room. Perry stomped after

them. Lois was still writing feverishly. As Perry stalked past her, Lois asked, "Perry, how many F's are in cata-strophic?"

"None," Perry growled. "What's the usage?"

Lois frowned at her pad. "This mysterious electro-magnetic pulse set a catastrophic event into motion, knocking out power during the highly touted —"

"Lois?" Perry said.

Lois looked up. "Yes?"

"This goes for everybody," he shouted after his depart-ing staff. "The story isn't the blackout. It's Superman!"

"But —" Lois began.

"In my office!" Perry snarled.

Clark sat at his desk in the bullpen. He slid his glasses down his nose and stared, with X-ray vision, through Perry White's closed door. His used his superhearing to eavesdrop shamelessly.

Lois stood before Perry's huge semicircular lacquered desk, arguing her point. "The story is the electromag-netic pulse, Chief. Every electronic device on the East Coast goes dark and —"

Perry leaned forward in his chair. "Lois, there are

three things that sell papers in this world: Tragedies, scandal, and Superman. I'm tired of tragedies and you're a rotten scandal writer. So that leaves *him*!"

Clark blinked as a handsome brown-haired man rushed through the door of Perry's office and swept Lois into a fierce hug.

Clark frowned. It was the man from the photograph on Lois's desk.

"Hi!" said a high-pitched voice beside Clark.

Clark looked over. The boy from the photo was looking up at him. He was maybe four or five, thin, with glasses. His thick brown hair flopped into his face.

"Hello," Clark said.

The boy popped an L-shaped tube into his mouth and breathed in. Then he shrugged. "It's an inhaler," he told Clark. "I have asthma. Who are you?"

"I'm Clark. Kent. An old friend . . . of your mom's. From before you were born."

Jason frowned. "Really? She's never mentioned you."

Clark's heart sank. "Never?"

Jason shook his head.

"Jason!" Lois called from the door to Perry's office. She raced over to Jason and swept him into her arms. "Weren't you supposed to wait for me in Daddy's office?"

Jason pouted a little. "Daddy's office is boring."

Lois looked over Jason's shoulder and seemed to really see Clark for the first time. "Clark," she said. "Welcome back."

Clark stared at Lois, suddenly confused. How should he greet her? Should he stand, offer a handshake? Hug her?

Lois leaned over and kissed him lightly on the cheek. "I see you've already met the munchkin," she said.

"Yeah," Clark said. "We were just talk —"

Lois turned to Jason. "Did you take your vitamins? Eye drops? Proventil? Poly-Vi-Flor?"

Jason nodded.

"He's a little fragile, yet," she explained to Clark. "But he'll grow up to be big and strong like his dad." She ruffled Jason's hair. "Won't you?"

Jason nodded again.

Clark said, "I saw you on TV in that —" He made a flying motion with his hand. "You're okay?"

"Oh yeah, it was nothing." She turned toward Perry's office. "Richard!"

Clark knew he had maybe a third of her attention. "Oh, and congratulations. On the Pulitzer. That's incredible."

"Yeah, can you believe it?" Lois rolled her eyes. "Richard!" she shouted. "So, I want to hear all about your trip! Where'd you go? What'd you see? Meet anyone special?"

Clark blinked. "Well, there's just so much. Where to begin really . . ."

The brown-haired man walked out of Perry's office. "You screamed for me?" he asked with a grin. He picked up Jason.

Jason hugged him. "Hi, Daddy!"

Lois turned to Richard. "Listen. I've got to run out. Can you take Jason to get his flu shot? And work some family magic to get your uncle to stop giving me a hard time about my article — please?"

Richard grinned down at her. "Again?"

Lois leaned up and kissed Richard on the lips. Clark shifted uncomfortably. He cleared his throat.

Lois turned to Clark. "Oh! Clark Kent, Richard White. Richard's the editor who's basically saved our international section. He's also a pilot, and he likes horror movies. And Clark is . . . well, Clark."

Richard put Jason down and shook Clark's hand. "Great to finally meet you. I've heard so much."

Clark glanced at Lois, surprised and pleased. "You have?" he asked.

Richard grinned. "Yeah. Jimmy just won't shut up about you."

"Gotta run," Lois said. "You heard Perry. Superman's back and Perry thinks I'm the only one equipped to give him a . . . he used the words 'an intimate story.'"

Richard raised his eyebrows. "So you're listening to him?"

Lois grinned. "Nope. I'm going to the power plant to look into the blackout. See ya!"

Richard called after her, "When will you be home?" But Lois was already gone.

Richard grinned. "She'll be like this until she solves the blackout mystery. Nothing will stop her. It's what makes her a brilliant reporter," he murmured.

He turned to Clark. "I'll be seeing you around the office. If you ever need me, I'm right over there."

He pointed to a large office next to Perry's.

Richard nudged Jason. "C'mon, kid. Say good-bye to Clark."

Jason smiled. "Bye, Clark,"

Clark smiled back. "Bye, Jason," he said.

Ten

Lex Luthor stopped in the middle of the Vanderworth's circular driveway and stared at the morning edition of the *Daily Planet*. The headline read: THE MAN OF STEEL IS BACK. Below was a photograph of Superman, looking handsome and noble as usual.

Kitty peeked over his shoulder at the photograph. "Hell-o!" she said appreciatively.

Luthor ground his teeth and growled.

Safe in Kitty's arms, Mrs. Vanderworth's tiny Yorkie growled back at him.

Luthor glanced at the dog with loathing.

"Isn't he cute?" Kitty asked.

Lex snapped the paper shut as a military humvee screeched to a stop in front of him. Grant, Riley, Stanford, and Brutus climbed from the truck.

"We got it, boss," Grant said. Brutus opened the hold, revealing a long crate.

"Put it on the yacht," Luthor ordered.

Brutus and Grant carried the crate into the main gallery of the yacht with Stanford and Riley trailing them. Luthor and Kitty, carrying the little dog, followed behind.

Brutus pried open the box, revealing a shiny brass rocket launcher.

"So what are we going to do, boss?" Stanford asked Luthor anxiously.

"*You're* going to modify it according to the plans I gave you and attach it to the stern," Luthor growled.

"No," Stanford said, "I meant about — *him*! Superman was supposed to *die* up there! Six months! That's how long it took me to get into the astronomical society. Another three to fake that sound transmission from Krypton and to leak the word to *National Scientific*. Superman's not dumb, boss. He'll trace all of that right back to me — and you!"

Luthor raised a finger. "Give me a minute!" he said.

He stared off into space, then at the items spread across his desk. Books on crystal growth. Varieties of crystals. A stack of *National Scientific* magazines.

Kitty put the little dog on the floor. The Yorkie whimpered, interrupting Luthor's concentration. Luthor hurled the newspaper at it.

The Yorkie dodged aside, sniffed the paper, then lifted his leg and peed on it.

Luthor glared at the dog. Then he saw the small headline on the back page of section A: WORLD'S LARGEST COLLECTION OF METEORITES ON EXHIBIT AT METROPOLIS MUSEUM OF NAT-URAL HISTORY.

Luthor picked up the smelly wet paper between his thumb and forefinger. He handed it to Stanford.

"You worry too much," Luthor told the younger man. Luthor turned to Kitty and growled, "And find that dog a nice home!"

Clark and Lois crowded onto the elevator with the rest of the workers heading home.

Lois stared up at the numbers absently, watching the floors count down. She didn't say anything.

Neither did Clark. He was watching her, a bit worried. During the past week, she had grown thinner and more distracted.

When the workers spilled out into the lobby and poured through the exit doors, Lois hurried along with them.

"Uh, Lois?" Clark called after her.

At the curb, Lois turned. "Hey Clark. How's your first week back at work?"

Clark shrugged. "It's okay. Kind of like riding a bike, I guess. You know — it comes back to you. Listen, since I've gotten back we haven't really had a chance to catch up. Would you want to —?"

"Hey, can I ask you something?" Lois interrupted. "Have you ever been in love?"

Clark opened his mouth. He didn't know what to say.

"Or at least . . . have you ever met someone and it's almost like you were from totally different worlds, but you share such a strong connection that you knew you were destined to be with each other? But then he takes

73

off without explaining why, or without even saying good-bye?" She paused. "Sounds cheesy, I know."

Clark thought a minute. "Well . . . maybe he *had* to go and he didn't know for sure how long he would be gone — a few weeks or forever."

At the corner, a traffic light turned green. A wall of cars raced toward them. Lois stuck out her hand. "Taxi!"

Clark stared down at his feet. "Maybe he wanted to say good-bye, but he couldn't find the guts to do it, because maybe if he saw you, even one last time . . . Well, maybe he was afraid that if he even looked at you just . . . once . . . he would never be able to leave." Clark looked at her directly. "Who are we talking about, anyway?"

"Nobody!" Lois waved her hand. "Forget I said anything. TAXI!" She whistled. Cabs zipped past.

"So . . . do you want to grab a quick bite? Catch up? My treat," Clark said.

"I'd love to," Lois said as she waved her arm frantically at the cabs roaring past. "But Richard took the car and it's my turn to cook dinner. Which means I've got just enough time to get back to the suburbs and order in Chinese food."

"Suburbs?" Clark asked. "You used to live —"

"We have a really nice place on the West River. You should drop in sometime," Lois told him.

"Count on it," Clark said. He took pity on her and whistled.

A cab screeched to a halt in front of Lois. "Wow. Thanks," she said. She climbed into the rear passenger seat. "312 Riverside Drive," she told the driver. She looked out the window. "G'night, Clark."

Clark sighed as the cab pulled away. "See you, Lois," he said softly.

Eleven

Superman flew over Metropolis. People looked up and pointed, exclaiming excitedly, "It's Superman! See? He *is* back!"

He flew east, over the city and beyond. The apartment buildings became houses and the city noises faded. He soared over the road that edged the West River, searching the houses that lined the shore for number 312.

He spotted the seaplane at the dock — the kind he knew Richard flew. There was a swing set on the back lawn.

With X-ray vision, Superman looked inside the house.

Upstairs were several bedrooms. An airy boy's room was cluttered with model airplanes and toy trains. Beyond that was the parents' room, with magazines and books piled beside the bed and clothes tossed carelessly over a chair.

He focused on the ground floor. There was Lois in the kitchen, pulling Chinese takeout from bags. Richard was setting the table with plates and chopsticks. In the living room, Jason was picking out "Heart and Soul" on a small electronic keyboard.

"Kung pao shrimp," Lois called.

"Mine," Jason shouted, running into the kitchen.

"Nice try, kiddo," Lois said. "No peanuts, no seafood, and definitely no wontons for you!"

She opened another box. "Here's yours," she said. "Plain rice and delicious steamed snow peas!" She scooped a portion onto his plate.

Jason rolled his eyes. He slumped back into the living room.

Richard frowned. "Why do we get Chinese food if he's allergic to most of it?" he asked.

"Because he loves the snow peas," Lois said, exasperated. "And I think we all prefer egg rolls over macrobiotic shakes."

"Macrobiotic — ICK!" Jason shouted from the living room.

Lois scooped a little of the shrimp onto her plate. She gave the rest to Richard.

"Lois, you're not eating. Or sleeping," Richard began. "Is something wrong?"

"Wrong . . . ?"

"I promised myself I'd never ask you about this — but now that he's back . . . your article . . . "

"'Why the World Doesn't Need Superman?'" Lois asked.

"No. No — the other one — from before we met," Richard said. "'I Spent the Night with Superman.'"

"Richard, that was just a title for an interview — your Uncle *Perry's* idea!" Lois sighed and looked at him directly. "It was a long time ago."

Richard met her eyes. "Were you in love with him?"

Lois smiled and began scooping out the rice. "He was Superman. Everyone was in love with him."

"But were you?"

Lois turned away to toss the empty containers in the trash. "No," she said. "I wasn't!"

She told Richard she didn't love me, Superman thought. But she *had* — once. Five years ago, they had loved each other.

It doesn't matter how Lois felt back then, Superman told himself sternly. *That was then and this is now. You left — you made your choice. And Lois made a life for herself without you. She has a son.*

He flew up — high and fast — trying to outpace his racing thoughts. On the very edge of space, he hovered and bowed his head.

In his mind, he heard Lois saying, "He was Superman. Everyone was in love with him."

And he heard Jor-El's voice, as clearly as if his Kryptonian father were standing before him. "Even though you were raised as a human being, you are not one of them."

So what makes me think I have the right to lead a normal human life? he asked himself.

He had come to Metropolis with his parents' admonitions ringing in his ears. His human father's belief that he had been put on Earth for a reason. Jor-El's be-lief that he would lead humanity to greatness.

For a while, he had done his best. The world had accepted him. Lois had loved him. He wondered why he had ever left.

Now he faced facts:

He *was* different — the last of his kind. And, he asked himself, was being different really all that bad when it gave him the power to help in ways no one else ever could?

If he wanted any kind of normal existence, he would have to live a lie. There were people who would want to exploit him for their own gain. Or threaten those close to him. So no one, not even Lois, could ever know Clark Kent was Superman.

I owe the people of this planet, Superman realized. *Not as a paragon who'll "lead them to greatness." But as one man who helps another because he's able.*

For days, he had held back. As the world cried out for help, he had tried not to listen. For their own good, he'd told himself. But that had been the cow-ard's way.

Now, he opened up his superhearing and heard — everything. A cacophony of jumbled noises. Some-where in the distance, a sonic boom roared. Alarms rang. Sirens blared. Traffic roared. Music played. People fought and laughed and talked and loved.

He focused his hearing more sharply, searching the city below for the cries of those who needed him.

Then, like a high diver, Superman plunged toward Metropolis.

Twelve

A UH-1 Huey helicopter settled on the roof of the First Metropolitan Bank.

Four men, masked and wearing dark clothing, leaped from its cockpit. They pulled out a crate, and a hulking giant of a man lifted out the eighty-five pound prototype XM214 squad-support machine gun. They set it on its tripod and loaded its 1000-round six-pack.

"We break in, we blow their safe, and we get out fast," their leader told them. "Cops know we're here — guards must have warned them — but dispatch said they won't have chopper support for at least ten minutes. They may send a SWAT team —"

"No sweat," said the giant. "I'll guard the chopper." He hefted the machine gun Hollywood-style.

"Blow the roof access door," the leader ordered.

The large thief opened fire, ripping the locking mechanism to metallic shreds.

"We're in," the leader announced. "Let's go."

&oo; &oo; &oo;

The two bank security guards had heard the chopper land on the roof and had notified the police. They knew that backup was on the way, but were sure it would come too late. Besides, protecting the bank was what they were paid for.

They were racing up the stairs when World War III seemed to break out on the roof.

"They're blowing the lock to smithereens," the tall one said. "You ready?"

His partner nodded.

They raced up the final flight of stairs, revolvers drawn. They threw themselves against the walls beside the splintered door. Then, guns held in a two-handed stance, they leaned out and fired. *BLAM! BLAM!*

They took the gunner by surprise, but their bullets

bounced off his flak jacket. The big man swung the machine gun at the guards and pulled the trigger.

A round burst from the barrel — enough to easily cut a man in half.

We're dead, the tall guard thought.

Then Superman dropped to the roof between the gunman and the guards. Bullets bounced off the S-shield on his chest and fell to the rooftop.

The would-be robbers pulled Glocks from holsters and opened fire as Superman stepped toward them.

∞   ∞   ∞

Ten SWAT officers burst through the shredded door, weapons raised.

The captain's jaw dropped and he lowered his gun.

"What took you so long?" the tall bank guard asked.

The SWAT officers stared at the helicopter. Its blades were spinning slowly, like a mobile twirling in the wind. Each bank robber had been wrapped in a different blade.

The captain's face broke into a grin. This could only

be the work of one person: Superman! He really was back in Metropolis!

⊷   ⊷   ⊷

Superman soared above the city again, looking for trouble.

In the theater district, at the corner of Carlin and Bog, he spotted it — a blue 1967 289 high-performance Mustang, veering out of control toward a sidewalk crowded with theatergoers.

The dark-haired woman inside the car leaned on the horn, clearly panicked. Through the top of the car, Superman could see her desperately pumping the brakes.

He landed in front of the vintage car and scooped its front end off the ground.

"Turn off the engine!" he shouted to the woman.

He heard a click and the engine shut off. He set the car down and stepped around to the driver's door. "Miss, are you all right?" he asked.

Kitty Kowalski stepped out of the car. Her black dress fit like it had been spray-painted on her body.

"My heart!" she exclaimed and grabbed her chest dramatically. She closed her eyes and, with a little gasp, fainted gracefully into Superman's arms.

Tourists pulled cameras, Mini-cams, and camera phones from bags and pockets. Dozens of people snapped hundreds of pictures.

When the barrage of flashbulbs had dwindled, Kitty's eyes fluttered open. "Heart palpitation!" she whispered. "I have a heart palpitation . . . and a murmur. And my back — I think I ruptured a . . . a cylinder."

Superman quickly scanned her body with X-ray vision. "I don't see anything wrong," he tried to reassure her.

Kitty fluttered her eyelashes, wrapped her arms around his neck, and moaned, "Please, take me to a hospital."

Superman shrugged. With Kitty Kowalski clutched in his arms, he rose into the air and flew toward Metropolis General Hospital.

It was ten minutes till closing when Lex Luthor and his gang, disguised as tourists, rushed into the Metropolitan Museum of Natural History and dashed toward the Hall of Geology.

Luthor stopped at the hall's entrance. "Stay here," he told Grant and Brutus. "Make sure we aren't disturbed."

Luthor, Stanford, and Riley strode toward a sign reading: A HISTORY OF METEOR SHOWERS.

Luthor hurried past a large meteor the size of a Volkswagen. He ignored ones the size of trashcans. Finally, he stopped before an ugly brown rock the size of a football. Its label read: ADDIS ABABA, 1978.

Luthor yanked it from the wall. An alarm sounded.

Several guards came running. As they rushed past, Grant and Brutus, Luthor's henchmen, knocked the guards unconscious with karate chops to the backs of their necks.

Nervously, Riley continued filming as Luthor pulled out a small hammer and tapped gently at the rock's exterior. Brown crust crumbled away, revealing translucent material that glowed an eerie green in the dim museum light. Kryptonite!

⊶ ⊶ ⊶

Superman landed outside the emergency entrance to Metropolis General Hospital with Kitty Kowalski in his arms. "All right, miss, we're here," he said.

Kitty's arms were around Superman's neck. She stretched one of them, just a bit, so that she could peek at her watch. *Just a little longer!* She smiled worshipfully up into Superman's face. "It's a miracle!" she said. "My back, my heart palpitation — healed! What did you do?"

"Nothing," Superman said. Nervously, he put Kitty down and tried to unwrap her arms from around his neck. "Nothing. I just —"

Kitty clung to him more tightly. "Call me Katherine," she murmured.

Gently, Superman removed her arms and stepped back. "Katherine, I really should be going."

Kitty checked her watch again and shrugged. "Of course. Places to go, people to save." She looked around. "I know this is so tacky, but do you want to grab coffee sometime?" She blinked. "Forget it. Forget I *ever* said that. Thanks for your help. Bye."

Kitty turned and swayed down the street on her stiletto heels. Superman frowned after her, puzzled.

Then, once more, he leaped into the air.

Thirteen

During the next eighteen hours, Superman seemed to be everywhere.

In Germany, he caught two window washers before they fell to their deaths.

He prevented the crash of a transport plane carrying supplies to a famine-starved region of Africa.

He lifted a cruise ship out of the path of a typhoon.

He blew out a fire on a tanker off the coast of Japan.

In Brazil, he saved a dozen families from rising flood-waters.

New stories were constantly appearing from news media around the world. It seemed as if Superman was on a nonstop world rescue mission. And that half the people on earth had a camera to record his appearances.

"It's like this on every channel," Gil said, staring up at the video monitors in the Daily Planet bullpen.

"All those people getting all those shots of him," Jimmy Olsen muttered, "and I have zip!"

◆◇ ◆◇ ◆◇

Clark sauntered into the bullpen, grinning happily. During his lunch break, he'd rescued a kitten from a tree, saved several lobster fishermen in Maine whose boat had overturned in a storm, caught a toppling crane from a building site in Houston, and blown out a wildfire near Los Angeles.

He joined Jimmy and Gil by the monitor, watching as two would-be robbers were led away by cops as a deli owner looked on.

A reporter asked the man, "Did Superman say anything?"

"He tried the hummus," the deli owner said. "He said he liked it. And Superman never lies."

Hiding a smile — it *had* been good hummus, and it *was* his lunch hour — Clark turned and headed toward Perry White's office for an after-lunch meeting.

Sighing morosely, Jimmy followed.

Lois was already sitting in one of Perry's plush leather visitors' chairs, staring glumly at the front page of a rival paper. A photo of Superman with a dark-haired woman in his arms took up the entire front page. The headline read: SUPER SAVE!

"So?" She tossed the paper onto Perry's desk.

"So? *So!* That's iconic imagery!" Perry leaned on his hands, glaring across the glossy surface. "And it was taken by a twelve-year-old with a camera phone. Olsen, what've *you* got?"

Reluctantly, Jimmy handed him a photo of the Metropolis skyline. Across it was a chalk-like blur.

Perry sighed. "Sit down, Kent. Olsen. Let's talk some half-time strategy."

Clark took the chair next to Lois. Jimmy backed toward the wall.

"Not long ago," Perry began, "Superman and the *Daily Planet* went together like bacon and eggs. Death and taxes! Now I want that bond back!"

He looked at Lois. "Lois, I don't know what you've been doing, but other female reporters have been waiting on rooftops, hoping to snare the next big Superman interview. And none of them have the history you two do."

"What?" Lois sighed in exasperation. "*NO!* Chief, listen to me. I've done Superman! Covered him — you know what I mean."

"Exactly!" Perry said. "That makes you the expert, so you're going to do him again."

"But there are a dozen other stories — the museum robbery last night for instance. Even Superman missed that one. He was too busy saving this . . . stripper."

Clark frowned. *What* museum robbery? When had *that* happened?

"And they stole —?" Perry asked.

"A meteorite," Lois said reluctantly.

"Boring," Perry said. "Gil can handle it."

"What about the blackout?" Lois pressed.

Perry pointed at Clark. "Kent? Blackout." He turned to Lois, arms folded. "Lois? Super. Man."

When Perry folded his arms like that, Lois knew it meant there was no way she could talk him out of it.

"Great. Thanks, Chief," she muttered and stormed out of the office. Clark leaped up and rushed after her. Jimmy stared after them.

"What are *you* standing around for, Olsen?" Perry growled. "Bring me one decent picture of Superman this week or you're a copy boy again!"

Clark followed Lois to her desk.

He started to apologize but Lois just held out a stack of files marked BLACKOUT.

"Take them!" Lois urged. "You wanted out of obits? Here's your chance!"

"Okay . . . but I'd hate it if this damaged our relationship," Clark said.

Lois blinked at him. "Relationship?"

She glanced at the TV screen where Superman was holding up a chain of twelve mountain climbers. She rolled her eyes.

Superman awakens, eager and nervous to find what remains of his home planet, Krypton.

Martha Kent lovingly cradles her long-lost son in the ruins of his ship.

Lex Luthor finds time to adjust his wig in between plans for world domination.

Jimmy Olsen surprises Clark with news about Lois Lane.

Perry White, editor in chief of the *Daily Planet*, is bent on getting the latest news on Superman's return.

Lois Lane, the paper's star reporter, is as determined as she is beautiful.

It looks like a model train set, but Lex Luthor has much more in mind than just playing with trains.

What malevolent scheme will Lex Luthor plot next?

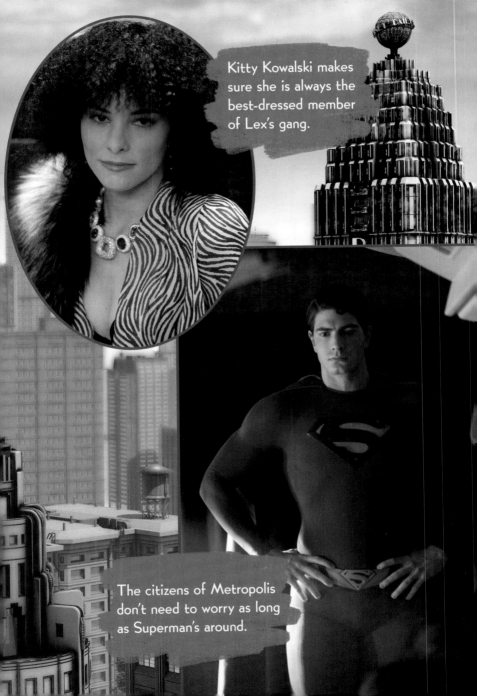

Kitty Kowalski makes sure she is always the best-dressed member of Lex's gang.

The citizens of Metropolis don't need to worry as long as Superman's around.

As Lois runs off, Richard and Jason smile at her steadfast pursuit of a hot story.

Superman and Lois finally have a private moment together on the roof of the Daily Planet building.

When Metropolis is struck by disaster, Superman is there to pick up the pieces.

Lex is not always the friendliest host to his guests Lois and Jason.

Lois is desperate to find a way to save Jason.

Superman has finally returned, and Lois Lane's back to covering the *Daily Planet*'s top news story.

"Mommy!" Jason ran up to Lois and hugged her legs. She smiled down at him and ruffled his hair.

Richard followed, holding up Jason's report card. "He got an *A* in science, but a *D* in gym, so we're doing something right."

Lois smiled over at him. "At least one of us is."

Richard noticed the stack of BLACKOUT folders Clark was holding and looked at Lois questioningly.

"It's Perry," Lois explained. "He just pulled me off the blackout and shoved Superman back into my life."

Richard studied Lois for a minute. "How about this," he said. "We'll stay late, get dinner — I'll help with Superman, and you and Clark can work on the blackout together."

"Okay," she agreed. "Yeah. That would be great."

"Is that good for you, Clark?" Richard asked.

Clark smiled. "Sounds swell!"

Kitty Kowalski stormed into the main cabin of the *Gertrude* and slapped Luthor's face, hard. "I was gonna *pretend* my brakes were out. Like we talked about. *Pretend!*" she yelled. "You didn't have to actually cut them!" She raised her hand to hit him again.

"Of course, I did." Luthor grabbed her wrist. "Superman could tell if you were pretending. He can hear your heart beat, watch your blood flow."

Kitty jerked her arm away and rubbed her wrist. "Did you get your dumb rock?"

Luthor nodded. He gestured toward a contour map hanging on the wall. It showed Metropolis and the Atlantic Ocean beyond. Twelve dark lines slashed across sea and land. A pushpin was stuck into the point where the lines intersected.

Kitty pouted. "What are those lines running through Metropolis and the ocean?"

Luthor smiled. "Fault lines. Deep cracks where the earth's crust is breaking apart. Now ask me about the pin."

Kitty folded her arms.

"That pin is where we're going," Luthor told her.

Grant's voice crackled over the speaker. "Mr. Luthor, Stanford's about to start!"

"Duty calls, Ms. Kowalski. We'll talk more about this later." Luthor left the room.

On the *Gertrude*'s upper deck, a rocket lay on a counter, its inner parts removed, leaving a hollow shell. As Luthor watched, Stanford carefully measured its inner compartment. Then he examined the football-sized meteorite. Most of its outer crust had been chipped away, leaving the glowing inner core.

Stanford picked up a small hammer and glanced at Luthor. Luthor nodded.

Stanford raised the hammer and brought it down sharply. A dozen knife-like shards splintered off.

Luthor picked out the largest splinter and shoved it into his pocket. "Continue!" he said.

Fourteen

"Darn!" Jimmy squinted at a series of digital pictures on his computer screen.

Clark walked across the empty bullpen and leaned over his shoulder. "What's wrong?" The screen showed a red and blue blur across the Metropolis skyline.

"I've been hanging out windows all week, trying to get a decent shot. But Superman just moves too fast."

"Keep at it," Clark told him. "He's got to slow down eventually."

CLANG!

Clark turned. Jason, wearing a trashcan on his head, had just careened into a metal desk. "RAAAAAAR! RRRRR!" he roared, like a giant monster, and kept on going. *CLANG!* He slammed into another desk.

Clark looked at the child with concern. "Jimmy, is he . . . okay?"

Jimmy grinned. "He's fine. A few weird allergies, asthma — but the kid's come a long way since he was born."

Clark raised his eyebrows questioningly.

"Miss Lane doesn't like to talk about it, but Jason was born premature. They weren't sure if he was even going to make it."

⊕ ⊕ ⊕

Across the bullpen, Lois leaned over a large, detailed map of the East Coast spread out across someone else's desk. She circled a location and wrote a number beside it. "If these times are right, it looks like the blackout spread from a specific origin point," she said.

Richard glanced up from Lois's computer, where he had been reading old Superman articles. "So with the superhearing, does Superman hear each sound by itself, or everything all at once?" he asked.

"Both." Lois plotted another coordinate.

"He's certainly a lot taller than I thought," Richard said thoughtfully.

"Six-foot-two and three-quarters," Lois mumbled.

"I love that he can see through anything. I'd have fun with that."

Lois smirked. "Anything but lead."

"I bet he —"

"Two hundred twenty-five pounds," Lois said. "Faster than a speeding bullet, invulnerable to anything but kryptonite. And he never lies."

Richard frowned. "Kryptonite?"

"Radioactive pieces of his home world." Lois jotted down another figure on her map. "It's deadly — to him, at least."

Richard looked at her speculatively. "Sounds like the perfect guy."

Lois shrugged and plotted another point on her map. She frowned. The times appeared to count down toward somewhere in Metropolis.

"Jason, it's getting dark. Let's get these intrepid reporters something to eat," Richard said several moments later. "Hey, Jimmy, want to come?"

"Why not?" Jimmy slouched over to Richard. "Even if I wait here all night, it's not like Superman is gonna show up and pose for the camera."

"RAAARRRRR!" Jason said, trotting out the door behind them. "Burritos!"

Sitting at his desk, Clark glanced over at Lois. Now that they were alone, he wanted to say something. But what?

Lois looked up at him. "So. Have you found a place to live yet?"

"No. Still looking."

Lois frowned. "Where've you been spending your nights?"

"Oh . . . here and there." He took a deep breath. "You know, Lois — I wanted to ask you about that article —"

Lois stood abruptly. "Hey, I'm going to run downstairs for some fresh air. Let's talk when I get back."

She snatched up her purse and everything inside spilled over the floor. Makeup. Tape recorder. Pack of cigarettes!

She glanced at Clark, momentarily embarrassed.

She shoved the tape recorder absently into her jacket pocket, scooped everything else into her purse, slung the strap over her shoulder, and practically ran for the bullpen door.

Clark lowered his glasses. With X-ray vision, he watched Lois get on the elevator. She wasn't going down. She was going up. All the way up to the roof.

Fifteen

Dusk in Metropolis was miraculous. Light fading from the sky. Flashing neon. Apartment lights winking on. Lois leaned against the rampart, gazed out over the city, and felt herself relax.

She pulled a cigarette from the pack in her purse, stuck it between her lips, and flicked her lighter. The flame flared near the tip of her cigarette . . . and died.

"You know, you really shouldn't smoke, Miss Lane," a voice said from overhead.

Lois yelped and looked up. Superman was hovering in the air, almost directly above her.

"Sorry," he said as he landed. "I didn't mean to —"

Lois straightened. "I'm fine. Really. I just wasn't expecting . . . you."

"I'm sorry," Superman added. "For leaving like

that." Lois started to answer, but he continued. "With all the press around, it didn't seem like the best time for us to talk."

Lois frowned, confused. Then she realized what he meant. "Oh, right. On the plane."

"I know some people are asking a lot of questions now that I'm back, and I think it's only fair that I answer . . . those people."

"So, you're here for . . . an interview?" Her voice rose with disbelief.

He nodded.

"Okay." She sighed. "An interview." She reached into her purse, looking for her tape recorder.

He looked her over. "Coat pocket," he said. "The tape recorder's in your left coat pocket."

Lois smiled — that was so like the man she remembered. She turned on the recorder. "Let's start with the big question. Where did you go?"

"To Krypton."

Lois frowned. "But — you told me it was destroyed. Ages ago."

"It was," Superman said. "But five years ago, as–

tronomers found a suggestion that other Kryptonians had survived. I . . . had to be sure."

"So — you just built a spaceship and took off?"

Superman smiled. "Actually, I grew it!"

Lois rolled her eyes. "Naturally. And what did you find?"

Superman hung his head. "Nothing — the astronomers were wrong. The planet had been blown apart. The explosion of Krypton's sun had irradiated the fragments. The closer I got, the weaker it made me."

"Kryptonite." Lois whispered the word.

Superman nodded. "I almost didn't make it back."

"Well, you are back," Lois said. "And everyone seems happy about it."

"Not everyone," Superman said. "I read an article, Lois — 'Why the World Doesn't Need Superman.'"

Lois looked at him defiantly. "So did a lot of people. Tomorrow night they're giving me a Pulitzer for it."

Superman looked at her intently. "Why did you write it?"

Lois clicked off the recorder. She looked into his eyes. "How could you leave me like that?"

Superman stared at her, momentarily caught off balance by the question.

Lois folded her arms, beginning to get angry. "This guy I work with says you left without saying good-bye because it was too unbearable for you. Personally, I think that's a load of bull."

Superman sighed. "Maybe he's right. I'm sorry I hurt you, Lois."

Lois stared out over the city. "You didn't hurt me — you didn't hurt any of us. You just helped us find the strength to take care of ourselves. That's why I wrote the article. The world doesn't need a savior."

"Lois? Will you come with me? There's something I want to show you." He held out his hand. "Please."

She faced him. "I can't be gone long." She kicked off her heels. She stepped forward and placed her feet on top of Superman's. She looked up at his face.

What am I doing? This is wrong, she told herself. She forced out the words, "You know my . . . um . . . Richard, is a pilot. He takes me up all the time."

"Not like this," Superman told her. He looked down.

Lois followed his gaze and gasped. While she had

been looking up at him, they had been rising smoothly into the air. They were fifty feet above the globe on the Daily Planet building and climbing.

Lois felt Superman's arms close more securely around her. She shut her eyes as memories flooded back. She had forgotten how warm he was. They climbed until the city was a grid of lights below.

"What do you hear?" Superman asked her.

"Nothing," Lois said. "It's quiet."

"Do you know what I hear? I hear everything," he murmured. "You said the world doesn't need a savior — but every day I hear people crying for one. I'm . . . sorry I left you, Lois. I'll take you back now."

Superman dropped toward Metropolis. Toward its thrusting towers and bright signs. Its noise and its rushing humanity. The Daily Planet globe sped toward them and then they were landing on the rooftop.

Lois looked into Superman's eyes. Their faces were inches apart. Their lips . . . Abruptly, Lois stepped backward, out of Superman's arms.

She raised her chin. "Richard is a good man. And you've been gone a long time."

"I know."

Lois picked up her shoes and walked back to the door from the roof. Halfway there, she turned. "So will I still see you? Around?"

Superman began to rise from the rooftop. "I'm always around. Good night, Lois."

"Wait!" Lois called after him. He hovered, eyebrows raised. "Never mind," she said. "Good night."

She turned and went inside.

⚬⚬   ⚬⚬   ⚬⚬

"Food!"

Clark looked up from the file he was studying. Richard, Jason, and Jimmy pushed through the swinging doors into the bullpen, carrying loaded paper bags.

Clark stared at Richard, who was joking around with Jason, making the boy laugh. Lois was right. Richard *was* a good man.

Clark rested his chin on his hand.

He *had* owed Lois an apology for leaving without saying good-bye.

He thought about their near-kiss on the roof, and

how Lois had pulled back. *Lois was mine before she was Richard's*, his heart cried. But that had been five years ago.

She had written that article, in part, because she had felt abandoned, but she had found the strength to move on. Now he would have to do the same.

Jimmy dangled a FatBoy Burger bag before Clark's nose. "Hey, Clark. Got your burger and fries right here!"

"Sorry, Jim," he mumbled. "Right now, I'm just not feeling very hungry."

Richard looked around the bullpen. "Where's Lois?"

Lois walked through the swinging doors in a daze. She blinked in the blinding glare of the overhead light.

"Hey hon — do you want the veggie wrap or the tofu burger?" Richard turned to look at her. Her hair was windblown, sticking out wildly around her head.

"What?" Lois said. She shook her head, as though trying to wake up. "Sorry. I'll have the veggie wrap."

Richard frowned. "Lois, where have you been?"

"I . . . was just on the roof. Getting some air."

"Tell the truth, Lois." Richard raised an eyebrow. "Have you been smoking?"

Lois tossed her INTERVIEW WITH SUPERMAN article onto Perry's desk.

Perry squinted up at her. "Is this real?"

Lois folded her arms. "It's real."

"How'd you find him?" Perry asked.

"He found me. So, about that blackout —"

Perry changed the subject. "Lois, this is the biggest night of your life, have you picked out a dress? Something snazzy —"

Lois let herself be distracted for the moment. "It feels a little weird, winning a Pulitzer for an article called 'Why the World Doesn't Need Superman,' when according to this newspaper, we do."

Perry leaned forward. "Lois, Pulitzer Prizes are like Academy Awards. Nobody remembers what you got one for. Just that you *got* one."

"But —"

"This night's for you, Lois. Just enjoy it. I'm sure Kent's on the blackout."

Sixteen

Superman flew through shimmering northern lights above a frozen landscape.

It had been five years since he'd come to his Fortress of Solitude. Now he needed to be among the artifacts of his home world, and get advice from the father who had sent him to Earth.

He dropped through a dense bank of clouds and landed before the massive crystal structure. It felt . . . dead. Abandoned. Wrong.

He rushed inside. "Father!" he shouted. No crystals flared with light. No voice welcomed him.

He stared at the main console.

The Master Crystal — which had traveled with him to Earth as an infant, and which contained the essence of his mother and father and all the arcane knowledge and power of Kryptonian science — was gone.

"I have it, Miss Lane!"

Jimmy raced across the Daily Planet bullpen, carrying a blue evening gown swathed in plastic.

Lois's desk was covered with a detailed map of Metropolis and its suburbs. She held up one finger, signaling Jimmy to wait. She said into the telephone, "Department of Water and Power, please."

Jimmy held up the gown and looked at her quizzically. Lois pointed to the rack beside her desk. He hung it there and rushed off.

"This is Lois Lane, from the *Daily Planet*. I was wondering if — Yes, Superman is very nice — but I was wondering if I could ask you a few more questions about the blackout . . ."

Jimmy reappeared, holding a dry erase board. On it, he had written: RICHARD'S LATE — TUX NOT READY AT CLEANERS. CAN YOU PICK UP JASON FROM SCHOOL?

Lois nodded and waved Jimmy away.

An hour later, Lois was sitting at her desk, wearing the blue evening gown. She was putting on diamond earrings as she talked to another power company official.

"So the West End grid went dark at 12:36, and midtown ten seconds later. And before that? Racine and Newtown. Right." She made dots on the map and wrote numbers beside them.

"And before that? In Hobbs Edge. You're sure." She marked another spot. "And nothing before that? Thank you very much."

She hung up the phone and stared at the map. She pulled out a compass and began drawing concentric circles, linking the dots where the power had gone out simultaneously.

She stood and studied the map. The rings made a bull's-eye, and the center of that bull's-eye was a Hobbs Edge property, right on the Hobbs River. She marked it with an X.

She looked up, as if coming out of a trance. The wall clock read 4:30.

"Ohmygosh! Jason!"

She snatched up the map and her purse and raced for the swinging doors.

⚭   ⚭   ⚭

Lois pulled the station wagon to the curb in front of Jason's exclusive full-day school. She spotted the teacher waiting with him outside the building.

Jason trotted to the car, opened the rear door, and climbed into his booster seat. "You were late," he said.

"Sorry, honey. I know."

Lois waved at the teacher and pulled into traffic. "Daddy's waiting for us at the office with your suit," she said.

Jason groaned. "I have to wear a suit?"

"Yep!" Lois glanced at the map spread out on the seat beside her, with its enticing circles and the X that marked the spot. "We're just going to make one quick stop first."

⚭   ⚭   ⚭

Jason stared out the car window at a huge, fancy house with a swimming pool. "Where are we?" he asked. "Is this the Pulitzer?"

"No, honey —" Lois's cell phone rang. She checked the ID. *Richard.* Calling to remind her she was running late. She tossed the phone into the glove compartment. *I'll call him back in a few minutes, once I'm on the road,* she told herself.

"Mommy just needs to ask the people who live here some questions and then we'll go." Lois climbed out.

"Can I stay in the car?" Jason asked.

"Not on your life," Lois said, opening his door.

Jason unbuckled his seat belt and climbed down obediently.

❧   ❧   ❧

Lois rang the doorbell. And waited.

"Mommy, who lives here?" Jason asked.

"We're about to find out," Lois told him.

No one came. Lois heard Vivaldi playing. "Come on. I think that music's coming from the backyard."

They followed the music to a yacht anchored out back. The *Gertrude*. Lois frowned. Why did that name seem familiar?

"Wow!" Jason said. "Are the people you want to see on that boat?"

No one was in sight.

"I don't know. Let's find out." They followed the music down the pier, climbed the ramp, and stepped onto the rear deck of the yacht.

I'll just find out who lives here, Lois told herself. *Then we'll head back to town. It won't take three minutes.*

"Are we trespassing?" Jason whispered.

"Yes. No. I mean . . . shhhh."

They climbed a flight of stairs and walked through a glass door to an interior corridor. The music was getting louder. Then suddenly it stopped.

Lois began trying doors.

The first one that opened led into a walk-in closet. It was lined with rows of suits and shirts and shoes. There was another door beyond it.

"Look, mom!" Jason pointed. "I like the curly one."

Lois turned to see what he was talking about — a

row of mannequin heads, each displaying a different color and style of wig.

"Oh, no." Lois backed toward the door. Now she knew who the yacht belonged to.

There was a rumbling noise from below. The room lurched.

The ship's moving, Lois thought. She grabbed Jason's hand. "Come on, we've got to get out of —"

The door at the other end of the closet opened. A bald man in a bathrobe stood there, with toothbrush in mouth. Lex Luthor raised his eyebrows. "Lois Lane!"

❧   ❧   ❧

Luthor's henchmen marched Lois and Jason to the main gallery. Luthor joined them. A dark-haired woman in a low-cut dress followed — the same bimbo, Lois realized, that Superman had rescued the other night. Luthor was definitely up to something.

"And what's your name?" Luthor asked, peering down at Jason.

Jason lifted his chin. "I'm not supposed to talk to strangers."

"Smart kid," Luthor said, turning to Lois. "But I'm not really a stranger, am I? This is like a little reunion."

"Beautiful ship," Lois said. "How'd you get it? Swindle some old widow out of her money?"

The dark-haired woman snorted. Luthor frowned. He signaled with his head and the woman left the room.

"Hey, didn't you get a Pulitzer for my favorite article — 'Why the World Doesn't Need Superman'?"

Lois glanced at her watch. "Not yet. Didn't you have a few more years to go on your double life sentence?"

Luthor smiled. "You know, newspapers are funny. The trial is always front page news — but they lose interest during the appeals process."

Lois looked around room. The name *Gertrude*. The dark-haired woman laughing at her crack about Luthor swindling a widow. "Wait a minute. This was the Vanderworth yacht. Gertrude's brother —"

"Is a federal court of appeals judge." Luthor shook his head in mock sorrow. "You know, Superman is good at catching criminals, but he's not much on Miranda rights, due process, that sort of thing."

"Speaking of process," Lois said, "did *you* have anything to do with the blackout?"

Luthor's eyes lit up. "Are you fishing for an interview, Miss Lane?"

"It's been a while since you were a headline, Lex." She pulled Jason toward her. "How about we turn the boat around, call a cab for my son . . . and then you can do whatever you want with me."

"Sorry, Miss Lane — we won't be turning around, but we do have time for that interview." Luther pulled a sheaf of papers from a slot on his fax machine and offered them to her. "Your tools?"

Seventeen

It was 6:30 p.m. The Daily Planet bullpen was nearly deserted when Clark stalked through the swinging doors.

The Crystal is gone, he thought distractedly. *And I don't have a clue who took it.* Blowing snow had covered any evidence.

Jimmy looked up from his desk, his expression desolate.

Clark came to a halt. "Jimmy! What's wrong?"

Lois and Jason were missing, Jimmy explained. Lois had picked Jason up from school at 4:45 . . . and vanished.

Clark hurried toward Perry's office, where Perry and Richard, both wearing tuxes, were pacing. "I heard the news," Clark said. "How can I help?"

"We've tried her cell, but there's no answer," Perry

said gruffly. "You're a reporter, Kent. Help Richard track her down!"

Luthor paced the *Gertrude*'s main gallery. "Miss Lane, what do you know about crystals?"

Lois leaned back on the leather couch and shrugged. "They make great chandeliers."

Lex dropped a book into her lap. "Open it. You'll see that crystals are like beautiful viruses . . . absorbing from their environment in order to grow."

Lois flipped through a few pages. When she looked up, Luthor was holding a large white crystal, about a foot long. It looked . . . familiar.

"This crystal may seem unremarkable, but so does the seed of a redwood tree. *This* is how our mutual friend in tights made his Arctic getaway spot. Cute, but a little small for my taste."

Luthor strolled over to a large world map hanging against the wall. He pointed to a new landmass off the coast of Metropolis. "This is more what I had in mind."

Lois frowned. "You're building an island?"

"Initially. But it will grow." Lex pulled down a second map. "In a short time, it will become a new continent, encroaching on the east coast of the United States and reaching nearly to Europe. For lack of a better name, it's New Krypton. An extinct world, reborn on our own."

"Why?"

"Land, Miss Lane. You can print money, manufacture diamonds, and people are a dime a dozen, but they'll always need land. It's the one thing they're not making any more of."

"No government will let you keep it."

Luthor smiled. "No government will be able to take it away. I'll have Kryptonian technology thousands of years beyond anything they could throw at me. They'll end up paying millions for a tiny piece of this high-tech beachfront property."

Lois got up to study the map more closely. "Your New Krypton is directly on a fault line. There'll be earthquakes. Thousands will die."

"Millions! Once again, the press underestimates me. The sad fact is, that spot is the best place for the crystal to grow. Any other location is just a tad too deep, too shallow — you get the idea." Luthor shrugged. "If you want to make an omelet, you have to break a few eggs."

Lois stared at him. Richard, Clark, the *Daily Planet* — Metropolis would be destroyed. It was unfathomable.

Luthor grinned maniacally. "Come on, Miss Lane. Say it."

"You're insane."

Luthor shook his head. "No. Not that. Come on. I know you want to. It's just dangling off the tip of your tongue. Say it!"

"Superman will never let you —"

"Wrong!" Luthor shouted.

He snatched a metal box from a shelf and opened it. A green glow lit his face.

He stuck the box right under Lois's nose. A green hollow cylinder glowed with an eerie light. "Kryptonite!"

Luthor snapped the box shut. "Mind over muscle, Miss Lane!"

Lois sank back on the couch.

Bored, Jason wandered over to the piano and began to pick out "Heart and Soul."

"You know, in your article, you referred to Superman as a savior. But you know what I think?" Luthor strolled over to the piano and sat down beside Jason. As the boy picked out the tune, Luthor began to play an accompaniment.

"I think Superman's a lost, lonely, little boy looking for a home," Luthor continued. "That's why he ran off looking for Krypton. And that's why he came back . . . to you. I think he needs us — more than we need him."

Lois frowned. "How would you know he went to find Krypton? He only just told me. It hasn't been published yet."

"Think, Miss Lane. How do you get a stray dog out of your yard? You toss out a bone."

Lois's eyes narrowed. "It was you! You faked that documentation. All that signals from Krypton junk. You tricked him. Made him leave." *Tore him from me. Broke my heart.*

Luthor shrugged. "Finding someone with the right skills and connections to plant that story wasn't easy.

Luckily the press doesn't check facts like they used to. And nobody *made* Superman do anything he didn't want to do."

Superman nearly died on that wild goose chase, Lois thought. *And now Luthor's going to use Kryptonian technology to kill millions. I've got to do something.*

Luthor was playing two-handed now, tune and accompaniment. Jason began to mimic him. Not perfectly. But improving rapidly. Luthor smiled down at Jason. And Lois knew, when the time came, Luthor would kill them both without a qualm.

Jason was now playing in perfect sync with Luthor, expertly copying Luthor's flourishes. Then Jason began to play faster, adding his own complexities to the tune.

Luthor gaped at him. Abruptly, he slammed his hands down, hard and discordant, on the keys. All music stopped.

He stalked toward Lois. "Who's his father?"

"Richard White."

Grant's voice broke in over the intercom. "Mr. Luthor, we're approaching the coordinates."

Luthor stared down at Lois. "You're sure?"

"Yes sir," Grant answered. "Latitude 39 degrees north, and longitude 71 degrees west."

Without taking his eyes from Lois's face, Luthor walked over to the mantle and lifted down the metal box. He walked over to Jason and opened it.

The eerie glow lit Jason's face. Nervously, the boy looked from the box to Luthor to his mother. Nothing else happened.

Luthor shrugged. He snapped the lid shut and stalked from the gallery, the metal box under his arm. At the door he snapped at the hulking Brutus. "Watch them. Don't let them out of this room."

Quickly, Lois wrote down: *39 deg N, 71 deg W*. She now knew where they were and what was going to happen. All she had to do was tell the world.

Eighteen

Metropolis was a glimmer of light on the horizon as Grant crouched on the aft deck, checking the assembly of a brass rocket launcher resting on a tripod. Swinging the camcorder, Riley followed Luthor and Kitty as they climbed the steps.

Luthor opened the metal box and removed the kryptonite cylinder. He handed Kitty the empty box and pulled the Master Crystal from his jacket's inner pocket.

Carefully, he inserted the Master Crystal into the sheath of kryptonite.

Luthor grinned. "This is gonna be good!"

∞   ∞   ∞

Lois paced the main gallery. She had to warn someone. There had to be a way!

The fax machine! she realized. *I can send a fax! If —*

Brutus looked bored with watching her pace. He drifted nearer to the piano, where Jason was once again playing "Heart and Soul." Jason smiled and moved over on the piano bench so Brutus could sit beside him.

"Go on, try it," Jason said. "It's fun! Look!" Jason showed him how to play the simple tune and after a while Brutus picked it up. Jason began to play the accompaniment.

Taking advantage of Brutus's inattention, Lois sidled over to Luthor's fax machine. She scribbled HELP US! LOIS LANE beneath the coordinates.

She slipped the paper into the outgoing slot. Quickly, she tapped out the Daily Planet bullpen's fax number, hoping Brutus and Jason's rousing rendition of "Heart and Soul" would drown out the beeps. She hit the send button. The connection was nearly instantaneous. The paper began to scroll through the machine.

Luthor inserted the bonded kryptonite and Master Crystal into the modified rocket launcher bolted to the aft deck of the yacht, and stepped back.

"Ready, boss?" Stanford asked.

Luthor glanced at Riley. "Ready?" Riley held up his camcorder. Luthor turned to Stanford and nodded. "Ready!"

BOOM!

The rocket streaked from the launcher. It arced through the air.

SPLASH! It hit the water.

Luthor trained his binoculars on the area where the rocket had disappeared.

Behind him, throughout the ship, the power flickered and died.

In the Daily Planet bullpen, Clark, Richard and Jimmy clustered around Lois's desk.

"She was working on a map," Jimmy said suddenly. "Drawing circles."

Richard frowned down at Lois's messy desk. "Where is it?"

Sliding his glasses down his nose, Clark quickly scanned the piles that covered her desk with X-ray vision. "It isn't here," he murmured. "She must have taken it with her."

"Bad sign," Richard muttered. "Maybe she left additional notes on her computer." He typed a few commands. The computer refused to let him in. "Blast! She has a password," he muttered. "Let's try — *Jason*. Nope. *Richard*. Not it."

Clark sighed. "Try *Superman*."

Richard typed *Superman*.

The screen unlocked.

And the power in Metropolis went off.

Thirty seconds later, it came back on.

From the pillars above them, the TV monitors blared the news — a temporary blackout had swept across the world.

"Uh-oh!" Richard muttered.

Luthor nodded with satisfaction as the power came back on. "Phase one is completed."

He braced himself on the aft deck and focused his binoculars on the ocean beyond, where the rocket casing would be plunging deeper and deeper, into the Hudson Canyon.

Meanwhile, within the rocket casing, the Master Crystal was growing, branching, melding with the kryptonite.

Luther checked his watch.

BOOM!

He smiled at the sound; it meant that the growing crystal had shattered its casing right on schedule. The crystal would continue to descend into the chasm until . . .

He checked his watch again, timing it.

3 . . . 2 . . . 1 . . .

WHROOOM!

An undersea blast lit the sea for miles.

Above the yacht, huge bolts of lightning flashed from sea to sky. Thunder cracked and boomed. Waves began to heave around them, tossing the ship as if it were a toy.

In his mind's eye, Luthor saw a sea of bubbles, as huge

cracks began to form along the sea floor, spreading out-ward. The cracks would turn into chasms as the sea above them lurched and roiled.

Then, deep within the ocean, Luthor spotted an eerie green glow as columns of crystal began to rise.

❧   ❧   ❧

As the lights blinked on in the main gallery of the yacht, Lois glanced at the fax machine. The message hadn't gone through.

"C'mon," Jason said to Brutus as the ship heaved and shook. "It's just a stupid storm." He started playing again. After a moment, Brutus joined him.

Thanks, kid, Lois thought. She reset the paper, hit re-dial, and held her breath, hoping that the music and the storm would, once again, mask the fax machine's noises.

After a flurry of beeps, the paper began to scroll through. The message got to HELP US. Then, once again, the fax machine cut off.

Lois frowned. The lights were still on! She looked around. Brutus was holding the power cord in one of his huge fists.

With the other hand, he grabbed Lois and tossed her across the room.

⚯   ⚯   ⚯

Jimmy Olsen recognized the fax tone.

He raced across the bullpen toward the fax machine. Maybe Miss Lane had sent it, he thought, though why she'd do that instead of call . . .

The fax machine spit out a message:

39 deg N, 71 deg W.
HELP US.

Jimmy laid the cryptic message down in front of Richard and Clark. "It just came through the fax," he said.

At the same time, Richard and Clark said, "They're coordinates."

"Twenty miles off the coast," Richard said. "Jimmy, call the coast guard. And tell Perry I'm taking my seaplane from Metro-Pier. Clark?"

"No thanks," Clark said. "I get airsick."

Nineteen

Clark waited beside Lois's desk while Jimmy rushed into Perry's office with the news and Richard dashed from the bullpen.

When both men had vanished, Clark ran for the elevators.

He forced open a door and leapt into the elevator shaft. Hovering in midair, he ripped his business clothes off, revealing the red and blue Superman suit beneath.

Superman flew up the elevator shaft. He blasted out the service door on the roof and soared into the sky above.

As he flew out to sea, he heard a rumble from beneath the ocean, as if the Earth itself was groaning. Then he heard a deep, sharp crack!

He stared down with X-ray vision. The seabed was splitting open.

For an instant, Superman looked longingly toward the deep Atlantic. Lois was out there. She needed his help.

But Richard was on the way. He could rescue Lois and Jason from whatever trouble they were in, Superman told himself.

He could see the fissure growing wider and lengthening, ripping straight toward the city and its innocent millions.

Superman turned and raced the crack back toward Metropolis.

Out in the Atlantic, the storm pounded Luthor's yacht. In the main gallery, anything not bolted down crashed from shelves or skidded along the floor.

A lurching wave flipped the yacht almost sideways, overturning the piano bench and sending Jason sprawling. Still dazed from being thrown against the wall, Lois tried to crawl to him.

The rocking of the ship slammed Brutus into the pool table, which was bolted to the floor. Pool cues clattered from a holder nearby. Brutus grabbed one of them. Fighting to stay upright, he raised the stick and lurched toward Lois.

"Mom! Move!" Jason shouted.

Lois rolled to one side and Brutus's blow missed her by inches.

As Brutus raised the stick again, the ship rolled nearly sideways. Behind him, the bolts that held the piano to the floor ripped loose. The massive instrument skidded across the floor and slammed into Brutus. Man and piano crashed against the gallery wall.

Lois reached desperately for her son. Jason was breathing in deep croaking wheezes. Lois fumbled in his pocket, found his inhaler, and helped him get it to his mouth.

Jason huffed in the medicine. Once. Twice. As the spasm in his chest began to ease, he could breathe again.

"Mom!" he choked out. "That man hit you!"

Lois hugged him. "He was a bad guy. But he can't hurt us anymore."

She pulled Jason to his feet and led him across the rocking floor. "You've been really brave and a huge help. I just need you to be brave a little longer."

She yanked open the door.

Riley and Grant were standing in the corridor outside.

Over Lois's shoulder, Grant could see Brutus lying behind the piano. He pulled a pistol and pointed it at Lois.

"The boss ain't gonna like this," Riley grumbled. "What do we do with 'em now?"

Grant spoke with Luthor over the intercom.

"The boss says lock them in the pantry. We leave the ship in three minutes!"

∞   ∞   ∞

Superman reached Metropolis as the massive crack ripped through the financial district. Beneath the street, steam pipes burst, sending manhole covers shooting into the air. The city was shaking, in the grip of a huge earthquake.

Terrified families stumbled from residential buildings

onto the sidewalks. People ran from shops and res-
taurants.

A giant crack split Shuster Street. A mother and her
baby daughter screamed as they fell into the gaping
chasm.

Then Superman was there, carrying them to
safety.

At the Daily Planet building, Perry White leaned
across his office desk, glaring into Jimmy Olsen's face.
"What do you mean, Richard went after Lois?"

The lights flickered and went off. "Great Caesar's
ghost!" Perry roared. "Not another blackout!"

On the streets below, hundreds of car alarms began
to shriek. Beneath the sirens' wail was a deep throbbing
rumble.

The Daily Planet building swayed violently. Books
and family pictures toppled from Perry's desk and
crashed onto the floor.

"I don't think *this* is a blackout," Jimmy said.

Superman tried to be everywhere in Metropolis at once — flying people to safety, carrying the injured to hospitals, preventing accidents, blowing out fires.

On the lower east side, two massive skyscrapers swayed, almost touching. In minutes, one would topple into the other and both buildings would smash onto the streets below, killing thousands.

Superman grabbed a crane from a nearby construction site. He propped it between the buildings. The crane bent, then held. Superman hoped it would hold long enough for anyone in the buildings to get to the relative safety of the next block.

∞   ∞   ∞

The yacht *Gertrude* had taken on water and was wallowing awkwardly between the waves. Soon she would sink.

From his walk-in closet, Luthor snatched up the case filled with his favorite wigs.

As he stepped out into the corridor, he heard Lois pounding on the pantry door. She was shouting angrily, "Luthor, let us out of here!"

Luthor grinned at her through the pantry door's decorative porthole window. Then he dashed up the steps toward the helicopter.

Minutes later, the chopper was in the air.

Another tremor shook Metropolis as the chasm ripped toward midtown. Wires suspending traffic signals snapped. Fire hydrants gushed water. Street lamps toppled.

Jimmy and Perry, along with a stream of others, rushed from midtown office buildings.

In the midst of the chaos, Jimmy pointed his camera, documenting the disaster. He looked up.

The Daily Planet globe housed the building's water tower. Water was leaking from it as it swayed violently. Then its narrow base snapped. The globe toppled sideways, bounced off the tiered upper floors, and plummeted toward the street.

The crowd uttered a collective scream.

From blocks away, Superman heard. He scanned

midtown with X-ray vision and spotted the falling globe. Faster than a speeding bullet, he flew beneath it, catching it before it could crush the people below.

Click . . . whirr! Click . . . whirr! Jimmy snapped the perfect iconic shots of Superman.

As Superman set the globe down on the street, the ground stopped shaking. All grew quiet.

Perry stepped forward. "Perry White, *Daily Planet,*" he introduced himself to Superman. "What's happening now? Is it over?"

Superman shook his head grimly. His superhearing had picked up a distant, ominous rumbling that signaled trouble yet to come.

This disaster was so huge, he realized, even at superspeed he could never save everyone in Metropolis. He would have to follow the cracks backward and stop the destruction at its source.

"I need your help," Superman said to Perry. "Call the radio stations. Ask them to tell people to find shelter away from buildings."

"How can we avoid buildings?" Perry grumbled. "This is a city!"

"Send people into Centennial Park," Superman ordered. He rose into the air.

"But — where are *you* going?" Perry asked.

For an instant, Superman hovered there. "If I don't stop this thing soon, there won't be a city."

Twenty

From the comfort of his hovering helicopter, Lex Luthor surveyed the Atlantic. The glowing crystal superstructure was growing rapidly, rising higher beneath the waves. Soon it would break through the ocean's surface.

Displaced water created a tidal wave that rolled across the sea, swamping the yacht.

"Good-bye, Miss Lane," Luthor muttered.

❦ ❦ ❦

Locked in the pantry, Lois felt the ship rock violently. She lifted her son high onto an empty shelf. "We're lucky the shelves have been bolted to the wall," she told him. "And that the bolts are holding."

Unfortunately, that's about it in the luck department, she thought as she climbed up beside him.

She felt the sudden plunge and roll as the ship sank beneath a huge wave. Water leaking from the ceiling and dripping down the walls showed her that the ship was underwater. She looked over at her small son, clinging bravely to the shelf supports, and her heart ached.

Her relentless curiosity, her recklessness, her stubborn refusal to give up, had made her the *Daily Planet*'s star reporter. And if, occasionally, it had plunged her into peril, only her own life had been threatened.

This time things were different.

I shouldn't have brought Jason with me, she thought. *I should have anticipated the danger. How could I have done something so irresponsible?*

⊶   ⊶   ⊶

The pantry was tilted now. Icy water half-filled the room. The door was on the wall rising diagonally above them.

Then the lights went off, plunging the small room into utter darkness.

Lois could hear Jason struggling to breathe. "Mom, I–I dropped my inhaler. I think it's in the water."

Lois groaned. She reached out, feeling around for it in the darkness, hoping the thing would float. Something bumped against her fingertips and she grabbed for it. The ship rolled, her hand slipped, and she tumbled from her perch.

Saltwater flooded into her mouth as she went under. She lunged and kicked, but her long dress tangled around her legs and dragged her down.

Then, above her, she saw a light. A hand plunged into the icy water and pulled her to the surface and toward the dry part of the room, near the now-open door. A face was lit by the glare of a flashlight.

"Richard! How — how did you get here?" she asked.

"I flew," he said. For a moment they held each other tight.

"You're wet," she said.

Richard grinned. "I had an inflatable raft on board the plane," he said. "But I still ended up in the ocean."

While Lois held the flashlight, Richard plunged into the water and lifted Jason into his arms. He felt in his pocket for the spare inhaler he always carried, and handed it to the boy.

Jason hugged him. "Thanks, Dad," he said.

"You should see what's going on out there," Richard said as he shoved Lois up the incline toward the open door. "Lois, what have you gotten yourself into?"

"Don't blame me! This is Lex Luthor's mess," Lois said. "We've got to warn the world."

"Warn them?" Richard said. "About what?"

With a metallic groan, the ship lurched violently.

"What's that?" Richard yelled.

"Grab onto something," Lois shouted.

—℃℃— —℃℃— —℃℃—

Lex Luthor's helicopter hovered above the ocean's surface. He saw the crystal mass rising . . . growing higher, till it reached the ocean's surface.

Beneath the yacht, a huge crystal grew. It speared the hull of the yacht and thrust the whole ship upward.

The yacht, already damaged, snapped in two. The bow broke away and fell back into the sea. The stern slid back into the water. At most, it would float a few minutes longer.

Luthor's eyes slid back to his growing island. In the twilight, he never even noticed Richard's small seaplane bobbing near the yacht, among the growing crystals.

The wrecked stern of the yacht, the part that housed the pantry, rocked violently.

Richard lifted Lois toward the open doorway. As the stern rolled in the waves, she could see the door begin to swing shut.

"No! she yelled, lunging for the door, trying to block it from closing. She knew that if it closed, they couldn't open it from the inside.

"Lois! No!" Richard shouted. "It's too heav—!"

The thick, metal door slammed down hard. Lois tried to brace against it but it bludgeoned her, and she slid, unconscious, into the water.

As Richard grabbed for her, the broken stern slid beneath the waves.

Water filled the pantry, almost to the ceiling. Richard fought to hold Lois and Jason up in a small pocket of trapped air.

We can't last long, he thought. At least they had the flashlight. Somehow that made waiting to die more bearable.

Its narrow beam shone up through the porthole.

Then Richard saw something moving in the darkness beyond it.

"Jason, hold your breath and hold on to me tight!" Richard ordered. "I think we're going to be okay!" He clamped a hand over Lois's nose and mouth and held his own breath.

The door above them tore away. Water rushed over them, but that didn't matter.

Superman had them in his arms and was rocketing with them toward the surface.

He carried them to the seaplane and helped Richard and Jason climb into the cockpit.

"You're . . . him!" Richard said.

Hovering outside the plane, Superman handed Richard the unconscious Lois. "You must be Richard," he said. "I've heard so much about you."

"You . . . have?"

"Is Mom okay?" Jason asked in a small, worried voice.

Superman scanned Lois with X-ray vision. He listened to her breathing and her beating heart. He smiled reassuringly. "She'll be fine!"

BOOM! A gust of wind hit the plane like a hammer. The water around the plane began to churn.

Crystal columns thrust up from the ocean, nearly surrounding them.

"Lois said this was some scheme of Lex Luthor's," Richard said. "But how could one guy do all of this?"

"I think I know," Superman said grimly. "Can you fly out of here?"

Richard frowned. "I can't take off in this!"

"No problem," Superman said. "I'll push. Just promise you'll take care of them — and that you won't come back. No matter what happens."

Richard nodded. "I promise."

Twenty-one

Superman flew over the new landscape — a slice of Krypton, rising in massive crystal pillars from the sea.

On top of the largest tower was a flat open space, the size of a football field. Crystal columns formed a circle around it. On Krypton, that configuration was called the Valley of the Elders. This was a near-perfect replica. Only the family crests were missing.

In its center, a structure had grown — a duplicate of Superman's Fortress of Solitude. Next to it sat an empty helicopter.

Superman landed beside it, hard.

The wind whispered through the crystals, sounding like ghostly voices.

Then he heard another voice, coming from inside the fortress-like structure. "See anything familiar?"

Lex Luthor strode from the duplicate fortress, followed by a familiar dark-haired woman.

"I see an old man's sick joke," Superman said.

Luthor smiled. "A joke?" He tsked. "I see my new apartment. And a space for Kitty, here. And my friends." He shrugged. "But no, you're right. It's a little cold. A little . . . alien. It needs that human touch."

Riley stepped forward, shoving his camcorder into Superman's face.

Superman's eyes began to glow. Heat zapped from them, and the camcorder melted into black slag. Riley dropped the hot oozing substance with a yelp.

Superman shook his head, trying to get rid of a sudden wave of dizziness. He was beginning to sweat. "I don't have time for this," he said. "You have something that belongs to me."

"You mean the Master Crystal?" Luthor asked.

As Superman tried to step past him toward the new fortress, Luthor slammed him in the mouth. Superman fell to the ground.

He touched his lip. It was bleeding. What was happening to him?

"Wake up, mommy. Wake up!"

Jason's voice, Lois thought. She opened her eyes. *Where am I? Oh, Lord.*

She sat up quickly, then grabbed her aching head.

"Hey, it's all right. We're safe," Richard said.

Lois looked around. They were in Richard's plane. But they *had* been on Luthor's ship.

"How?" Her voice made barely a croak.

"Superman," Richard said.

Lois frowned and looked around. "Where is he?"

Richard glanced at her. "He went back to stop Luthor."

"Richard, we have to turn around," Lois said, panic rising in her voice.

"What? Why?"

"There's more to Lex's plot than just growing an island," Lois said. "Those crystals have been tainted with kryptonite. Unless we help him, Superman could die."

Richard looked at her, and then at Jason. Jason nodded.

Richard turned the plane back toward New Krypton.

In the heart of New Krypton, Luthor stood over the fallen Superman.

"I didn't send you off to Krypton just to have you come back and stop me now," Luthor said.

So it was Luthor, Superman realized. *He must have planted that story. But . . .*

"Why?"

"You robbed me of five years of my life," Luthor said. "I wanted to rob you of all of yours. Unfortunately, you didn't die there."

But I did lose years, Superman thought. *And any chance of a life with Lois.*

With enormous effort, Superman focused his X-ray vision and looked around him. Growing in and among the crystals, he saw deep veins of kryptonite.

Luthor pulled his foot back and kicked Superman in the gut. "Fly!" Luthor kicked him again. "Come on! Fly!"

Kitty Kowalski covered her eyes.

Summoning the remnants of his X-ray vision, Superman looked past Luthor at the newly created fortress.

Deep within the console, he could see his father's Master Crystal. But it, too, was surrounded by deadly kryptonite. Then his X-ray vision blurred and faded as his powers vanished. The ghostly whispers of his ancestors grew louder.

Luthor stood over him. "These crystals will grow throughout the earth. Kryptonite will poison everything," Luthor said. "You can't go back to Krypton . . . and soon you won't be able to live on Earth. If you live at all!"

Superman crawled toward the edge of the monolith. He reached the rim and peered over. The drop to the sea seemed almost endless.

Luthor reached into his pocket and pulled out the knife-sharp sliver of kryptonite that Stanford had chipped from the meteorite mere days ago. He raised it high, and then plunged it into Superman's back.

Superman screamed as kryptonite radiation burned through his body. And Luthor stepped back to watch him die.

But Superman still struggled forward. Then, with a

final, mighty effort, he threw himself off the cliff and into the sea.

Luthor stood on the cliff's edge, watching as Superman sank beneath the waves. Smiling, he raised a hand in a mock farewell. "So long, Superman."

Twenty-two

Tumbling and spinning in the turbulent water, Superman opened his eyes. Crystals were growing toward him from every direction. All were glowing green from embedded kryptonite.

He reached behind his back, trying to grasp the shard buried there. The movement was agony.

He kicked for the surface. But a mesh of crystal had already begun to grow around him. And he realized the transplanted crystals of his home world were going to be his tomb.

⊷　⊷　⊷

Richard piloted his seaplane toward the island of towering crystals.

Jason had his nose pressed against the glass. When

they were almost on top of the island, Jason pointed down at the water right below.

"I see him. Land here! Mom —" He turned to Lois excitedly.

"I don't see anything," she said. "Jason, you're sure?" Jason nodded.

"Put it down here!" Lois said.

❧   ❧   ❧

The plane dodged emerging crystals as it skipped across the water. Lois forced open the door.

"Lois," Richard yelled. "What are you doing?"

"I see him," Lois shouted. "There's no time!"

She dove from the still-moving plane and plunged into the ocean. Superman was trapped not far below. His arms were up as if he were reaching for the surface. But his body was nearly encased in crystal.

Lois swam deeper.

She grabbed Superman beneath his arms. Bracing her feet against the encroaching crystals, she pulled and tugged until he slid free.

Lois surfaced, gasping, with Superman wrapped in her arms.

Balanced on one of the seaplane's pontoons, Richard reached down to grab his cape.

Together, Lois and Richard lifted Superman into the plane and lay him on the floor in the small cargo hold. Lois bent over him, slapping his face.

"Come on! Wake up!" she ordered him. *He looks terrible,* she thought.

"Kryptonite . . . ," she heard Superman mumble. "Kryptonite in the crystals. Back . . ."

"You can't go back," Lois murmured. She turned to Richard. Over the rumble of the motor, she shouted, "We have to get him away from here!"

"I'm trying!" Richard growled.

Richard was trying to gain enough momentum to lift the plane into the air. But the water was too choppy and he had to keep swerving to avoid the crystal structures that burst from the water like spears, barring his way.

"That way, Dad!" Jason said, pointing to a narrow gap.

"Good call!" Richard said. If they could make it

through, they'd be in open water. "Seat belt!" he shouted.

Jason strapped himself in.

They squeaked through by inches. Then they were in the air.

"Mom," Jason said. "When Superman said *back*, I think he meant —" Jason pointed at his own back.

Lois frowned. She rolled Superman over and pulled aside his cloak. She saw it then — a shaft of kryptonite, embedded near Superman's spine.

Lois grabbed the large splinter and pulled. It slid, like a dagger from a sheath, leaving a deep indentation in his flesh. There was no blood. The punctured skin looked blackened, as if it had been burned.

Lois rushed to the door, forced it open, and hurled the kryptonite into the sea.

Superman opened his eyes. "How . . . did you find me?" he croaked.

"Shhh!" Lois knelt beside him. "You're hurt."

Superman struggled upright. "I'll be all right, now." He looked over at Richard, in the pilot's seat. "You promised you wouldn't come back."

"I lied." Richard smiled wryly.

Superman stood upright in the cabin, bracing himself against the wall. "I have to go back."

"No!" Lois protested. "You'll die if you go back."

Superman pushed the cabin door open. Wind poured into the plane. He turned and looked into Lois's eyes.

"Good-bye, Lois," Superman told her. He leaned backward into the wind. And *WHOOSH!* He was gone.

Twenty-three

The sun had not quite set. There was enough solar energy in its slanted rays to partially recharge his powers. Enough, at least, to let him fly.

He soared straight upward.

Below him and off to the east, New Krypton was huge and still expanding. It was hard to comprehend the damage Luthor had already done.

Superman flew higher still. Up into the stratosphere.

There he hovered, basking in bright sunlight until it had completely recharged his body's energy cells. Finally, when he had regained his full strength, he arced backward and dove straight down toward the sea.

Superman entered the atmosphere with such speed and power that the air around him ignited and he glowed bright as a shooting star.

His eyes blazed like a furnace as he fired a blast of heat vision that vaporized the clouds below, then hit the ocean's surface. The sea began to boil and mist.

Superman plunged through the superheated water to the ocean's floor. Using his heat vision to melt the sea floor into liquid magma, he drove deep into the ground.

He melted the rock to liquid as he swam, creating a magma-filled tunnel through the very crust of the Earth. He knew that the force of his passage would open massive rifts in the ocean's floor around the roots of Luthor's island. And that geysers of bubbles and gas would explode from the crevices, as the ocean floor was literally split open.

He was counting on it.

⊷ ⊷ ⊷

Standing on the surface of New Krypton, Luthor felt the ground tremble. He looked around, puzzled, and saw the horizon was sinking.

New Krypton was rising into the air.

One of the enormous crystal monoliths nearby began to crack.

"No!" Luthor said.

Kitty grabbed his arm in alarm. "Lex, what's happening?"

The monolith shattered at its base.

"Move!" Luthor shouted. Luthor, Kitty, and his henchmen dove out of the way as the huge crystal fell, shattering the fortress.

Behind the henchmen, a second monolith wavered and cracked. It fell on top of Luthor's thugs, burying them completely.

Luthor shoved Kitty toward the chopper. "Get to the helicopter! Now!" Kitty ran for her life. And Luthor ran with her.

They leaped inside the helicopter and Luthor started the engine.

He stared out the window, watching in horror as small cracks and fissures began to form beneath them. They had to get airborne.

The helicopter lurched and dropped. *Too late!*

Luthor thought, as the ground beneath the chopper crumbled away.

They fell into a deep chasm.

Then the engine caught and *VROOOM!* Luthor and Kitty were soaring safely into the sky and off to the west.

⊷　　⊷　　⊷

Once clear of New Krypton, Luthor turned the chopper around and hovered. He stared out the window in a horrified daze, as his new real estate venture rose from the churning ocean, higher and higher until its base cleared the ocean's surface.

The base was encased in a massive chunk of brown, rocky earth. Normal earth. Superman was a mere speck beneath the massive structure. But as he pushed, the island rose even higher.

⊷　　⊷　　⊷

Richard had circled the plane around.

Through the cockpit window, they watched, stunned, as Superman pushed the island even higher.

"Wow!" Jason said. "That's awesome!"

Lois held her breath as water sluiced from the mass of crystal. She could see that Superman had tried to use normal rock as a shield to protect him from the kryptonite. But it wasn't working.

Even as she watched, giant chunks of the darker earth broke off and splashed into the ocean far below. Exposed patches of the island's base glowed an eerie green.

Superman had known that might happen. That's why he had needed to move so quickly. Why he had to *keep* moving, while he still could.

Summoning all his strength, he forced the island higher. It was the hardest thing he had ever done.

Up . . . up . . . through the storm clouds.

More rocks fell away, revealing more layers of kryptonite.

Superman could feel the radioactive energy burning through his skin, into his nerves, sapping his strength.

I have to hurry, he thought. *Higher. Faster.*

He gritted his teeth and pushed on.

In the thin air of the stratosphere, he almost lost his grip. He cried out — in anger, in agony — and he pushed that monstrous mass higher.

Through the mesosphere . . . into the ionosphere. And out into space.

Once he flew above the shadow of the Earth, sunlight bathed his body, lessening the poisonous drain of the kryptonite, if only slightly. And it gave him the last bit of power that he needed.

With a primal roar, he used his final reserves of strength to hurl New Krypton toward the sun.

Along with the island, the Master Crystal that created it would be destroyed. His last tie with Krypton — all communication with his Kryptonian heritage — would be broken. Finally he would be a child of Earth alone.

The Crystal would burn . . . as he would burn.

Superman's eyes drifted shut and he fell, unconscious, back toward Earth.

Twenty-four

Like a shooting star, Superman plunged toward Metropolis. Wreathed in flames, he tore through the clouds that shrouded the city, lighting them with a fiery glow.

People pointed and stared, or turned and ran in terror.

He slammed into Centennial Park. The massive explosion knocked over trees and sent debris hundreds of feet into the air.

The noise was followed by an unearthly quiet. In the center of the park, smoke and steam rose from a scorched and charred crater ten feet deep.

A middle-aged policeman was the first to approach the crater. He leaned over and looked into it. A younger cop soon joined him.

"It's Superman," the young cop said.

"He saved the city," the older man agreed. "Somehow, he stopped the earthquakes. But at what cost?"

"You don't think he's dead?" a young woman asked, peering over his shoulder. Curiosity was beginning to draw a crowd.

"Naw!" the old cop said, reassuringly. "He can't be dead. He's Superman!"

The young cop nodded. "Yeah! He must've been in a real hurry to get home."

The crowd murmured in assent. "He's right!"

"Metropolis is Superman's home!"

"It's where he belongs."

A burly man said, "You think the ground is cool enough, we can go down there and haul him out?"

A young woman in a nurse's uniform nodded. "And get him to a hospital."

"All he needs is a little sunlight," an old woman told them, confidently. "He'll be just fine in the morning."

The next morning, Lois was looking at the front page of the *Daily Planet*. Richard sat on a corner of her desk as Jason dashed through the bullpen, wearing a red towel tied around his neck.

"I'm Superman!" he told Clark. "I saved the world!"

Clark gave him a thumbs-up. "Good going!"

Jason grinned back.

The headline screamed: SUPERMAN SAVES THE WORLD. Below was Lois's byline, the beginning of her article, and a huge picture — Jimmy's shot of Superman catching the Daily Planet globe.

"Cool, huh?" Jimmy said.

"Superman saved the world . . . blah-blah . . . !" Lois read. "Really works with your picture." She turned to Clark. "Nice article on Superman's activities during the earthquake, Clark."

"Thanks," Clark said. "Perry's finally taken me off obits. He —"

"Luthor got away, though," Lois interrupted. "I wonder where he went." She tossed the paper on the desk — it held *yesterday's* news — and stared off into space.

She leaped to her feet. "I've got an idea. I might be home a little late," she said, turning to Richard. "Can you do dinner?"

169

Before Richard could answer, she was through the swinging doors and gone.

Richard grinned over at Clark. "*My* call? Luthor doesn't stand a chance!"

Superman flew over Metropolis. The earthquake had shaken the city, but the damage could have been worse. Though he was still drained from his ordeal, he didn't want to rest. There was too much to be done.

He helped construction crews shore up the buildings he had propped up with the crane.

He flew injured people to hospitals.

He carried pets from damaged buildings.

He helped the Red Cross deliver supplies to the people who needed them.

And, mostly, he was happy.

He had saved Metropolis — and a good portion of the Earth. And in doing so, he finally understood that belonging wasn't a matter of where you came from. It was the choices you made. It was being comfortable in your own skin. But mostly, it was what you did to help other people.

He had heard the people standing over him as he lay in that crater. Their gratitude. Their willingness to help him. Their faith in him. Their certainty he belonged to them.

In turning from Lois to save Metropolis, he realized, he had made his choice. He would always love her. But she belonged to Richard now.

While Superman belonged to the people of Metropolis . . . and the world.